Shame's
Evidence

SHAME'S EVIDENCE

John Lenore

Sawmill Ballroom Publishing

Eugene, Oregon

Published by Sawmill Ballroom Publishing

29251 Hamm Road

Eugene, Oregon 97405

USA

ISBN 978-0-9799816-4-7

To Joy

Acknowledgements

I would like to thank Joey Blum at Sawmill Ballroom Publishing and Bill Giacalone for their participation in the creation of this book.

A special thank you to Tracy Robert and The Lord (not necessarily in that order) without whose involvement this book would never have been written.

PROLOGUE

THE ROTARY DOORBELL cragged her arrival when she twisted the pitted brass knob at forty Washburn Place. The pastor welcomed her in.

"Would you like something to drink? Some *soju*? I have *makguli*."

She demurred with, "No, I don't have much time," leaving her suede Italian flats at the front door. She walked directly to the bedroom at the end of the hall, the faded and scratched hardwood floor creaking beneath her feet with each step.

His well-kept room was not large; just large enough for his bed, desk, and brown La-Z-Boy recliner with a threadbare towel covering a well-worn leather seat. On the wall above his bed, framed pictures of his grown son and *hanbok*-gowned late wife stared down at him. Socks still on, he eased all the way back in the chair lifting the footrest and closed his eyes.

She dug out a foil strip of two condoms and a small zip-lock bag from her tweed Hermes handbag, its oversized gold buckle glinting the ceiling lamp's light. She opened the flaps of his robe, left side then right, tore open one of the foil packets and unrolled the condom over his penis. The pastor remained silent and prone on the chair.

Smoothly as a molting mink, she wriggled out of her panties and positioned herself over him. She lowered and raised herself methodically over his penis staring expressionlessly at him while he made small grunting noises. When the grunts became snores, she lifted herself off and with latex-gloved hands removed the condom and placed it in the plastic baggy. She cleaned his penis with a baby wipe then put that too in the bag along with the latex gloves.

She opened the second foil packet and unrolled the condom over his still pharmaceutically-erect penis, lowered herself onto it and closed her eyes. This time it would be for her.

When she finished, she removed the condom, placed it in the baggy with the other items, stashed it in her bag, restored her clothing, switched off the light and left.

CHAPTER 1 ALONE

CARTER BRAND ACCELERATED out of Minneapolis-St. Paul Airport short term parking and headed towards the exit to route 5. He slowed the silver-grey Prius to a crawl and hesitated just before leaving the airport unsure of whether to head east and home or west to Sunday service at Gethsemane Church. Not twenty minutes earlier he had said goodbye to Hannah with an emotionless hug and a peck on the forehead before she passed through security on her way to her sister's home in Los Angeles.

They refused to consider themselves officially separated as that status inevitably leads to divorce and neither of them was ready for that. Together five years and still childless, the passion faded first, followed by affection, leaving just the customary and contractual obligations of marriage.

Carter inched the Prius ahead in pace with the traffic's fitful flow, his thoughts drifting to early memories of Hannah. She was authentic, spontaneous, trusting to a fault and possessed a heart and soul that somehow had escaped corrupting influences of modern Korean and Western societies. Carter adored her like George Burns famously loved Gracie Allen with her charming not-as-dumb-as-she-sounds personality.

But after a while, her mangling of the English language and almost complete ignorance of even the most familiar Western popular culture references became tiresome, putting more and more distance between them. Though his *bon mots* were rare, he often wished Hannah would respond with something more than a blank stare.

With Hannah just gone, Carter already found himself adrift without routine. Since they were married, Sunday had been church day and Hannah, being a devout Christian, had taken the religious lead. They had found a Korean church where the services were given both in Korean and English with the Korean services simultaneously translated into English through wireless headsets allowing them to worship together.

Carter had developed a deep appreciation and respect for Gethsemane Church's Pastor Choi who preached from the heart with greater benignity than most of the Bible-thumping mid-western Methodist ministers with whom he had been acquainted in the past. Choi had an assuring smile and a peaceful disposition that could put even the most contentious soul at ease. He was human and never failed to remind the congregation that like Jesus on earth they were human too, with all the faults and shortcomings that are part of human character.

The heavy traffic trickling out of the airport kept the hybrid's engine fixed in its all-electric mode as Carter inched silently down 34th Avenue. The source of the bottleneck became apparent as he passed Fort Snelling Cemetery where rubberneckers gawked in magnetic repulsion at a pack of dogs tearing the flesh of a fallen deer. The lead hound stood guard, barking at the pausing cars, bloody fangs bared.

Ten minutes later, and ten minutes into the service, Carter cruised for an empty space in the crowded church parking lot. His year-old Prius stood in stark contrast to the numerous Mercedes, BMW and Lexus SUVs and vainglorious ethos of much of the congregation's membership.

He parked next to a spotless Hyundai and walked across the parking lot towards the rear entrance of the church. Carter could hear the muffled sounds of the choir growing louder as he climbed the staircase to the sanctuary. At the doorway, Elder Suh handed him a copy of the service program asking, "Where is your wife?" in passable English.

"She is visiting her sister," Carter replied respectfully, relating just enough information to avoid conversation. Carter could see that the pews were filled to capacity when Elder Suh opened the sanctuary door for him with a row of folding chairs arranged in a line along the back wall to accommodate the overflow.

Words to the hymns in English and *hangul* were usually projected in PowerPoint on a screen to the right side of the pulpit, but that morning the words were displayed in *hangul* only and the choir sang Korean versions of hymns which Carter could follow if the tempo was not too fast. Hannah had taught him to read the phonetic Korean writing, even if his comprehension was very limited.

In order to completely understand Pastor Choi's sermon, he would have to listen to the translation by radio. Carter exited the sanctuary, bowed to a greeter and requested a pocket radio receiver from a smiling female *chun-do-sanim*.

He flicked the switch to make sure it was working and headed for the balcony stairs.

The balcony was almost completely filled with just a single seat vacant on the far left side of the back row. From there, he could look down on the congregation, choir, musicians and the pulpit. His seat was so far back he found himself focusing not on the pastor directly but on the projected video image of him displayed on the screen after the choir and PowerPoint had finished.

American Presbyterian and Methodist missionaries arrived in Korea in 1884, but Christianity did not really flourish until the Japanese occupation in 1905 when many who had converted to Christianity martyred themselves rather than surrender their faith or their country. Like other areas in the world where Christianity was introduced, the faith was overlaid with existing traditions and traveled with Koreans when they immigrated to the United States. A carryover of this blending of American and Korean Christianity is the unique way many Koreans pray called *tongsung gido.*

The first time Carter experienced it - and it can only be experienced - was during a Wednesday night service given for the benefit of recent Korean immigrants. He remembered that near the end of the pastor's introductory prayer, the music grew louder and louder until it reached a crescendo at which point the pastor shouted *"Joo-yaah! Joo-yaah! Joo-yaah!"* signaling the assembled members to begin simultaneous, loud, rapid, passionate prayer. Carter's hair had stood on end as he looked left and right observing people pleading, beseeching, and crying for God's grace. He had wanted to join in but found he could not. Perhaps he could not have thought of so many things to pray about so quickly, or maybe he wouldn't have been able to move his lips that fast even if he could have found the words, or maybe he just would have felt strange doing it. In any case, he had simply bowed his head respectfully and glanced over at Hannah, her hands clenched together in intense prayer, tears streaming down her cheeks.

On this day, Pastor Choi's sermon followed the reliable theme of unbending faith in God using the venerable Bible verse Genesis 22:9. What could compare with the faith to kill your eldest son simply on God's command?

Jeannie Park-Reed translated each line with just the briefest delay from the time it left Choi's lips. She had the most unusual accent which sounded to Carter's ears like a smooth homogination of the local accents from all the places he understood she had lived since arriving in America from Seoul when she was just a teenager: Seattle, Boston, New York and finally Minneapolis. Her speech gave no betrayal of her native Korean, unlike so many recent immigrants who, he discovered, find it almost impossible to end English sentences without tacking on a vowel or two. It wasn't quite like any regional American accent. From months of listening to her translations, Carter could tell "JPR-speak" anywhere and that morning Carter found Jeannie Park-Reed's subtle syllable warping particularly adorable.

The weekly announcements were nearly complete when a man of about forty stood in the aisle waving a notebook and shouting at Pastor Choi in Korean. From his balcony vantage point, Carter could identify the man as Dr. Kang, a man with whom he had limited dealings but, with his heavy eyebrows and perpetual tan, even in the dead of winter, had a face he could not forget.

In the sanctuary below, Kang continued his verbal attack, becoming more animated by the moment. An elder stood up and consumed with anger shouted, *hajima*! which Carter understood from hearing Korean moms discipline their kids to mean "Stop that – now!" A woman rose to defend the pastor then another woman joined the argument to support Dr. Kang.

Carter was as appalled that there could be such behavior in a church service as he was compelled by his professional curiosity to find out what was going on. He turned up the volume wheel on the translation radio but heard only static. Meanwhile, the altercation below grew louder with more and more members joining the fracas. Carter dashed downstairs to the translation room just as Jeannie Park-Reed was locking the door.

"What was that all about?" he asked. "And what happened to the translation?"

"Wasn't worth translating."

"Well, can you give me a hint, just the gist of it?"

Jeannie pocketed the keys and through an abstruse smile said, "Forget it, it's a Korean thing."

When a Korean tells an American "It's a Korean thing" the subtext is often "None of your business." But Carter could not forget the image of Dr. Kang's vitriolic, notebook-waving, public tirade.

He had had a brief encounter with Kang during church fellowship time a few years back while discussing the issue of homosexuality. Kang argued forcefully that homosexuality was an unforgivable abomination and rattled off in quick succession a good number of biblical verses to support his case. After his philippic had ended, Carter opined, "I would really like to hear what a gay Christian has to say," causing Kang to immediately slam down his Bible and storm away mumbling to himself about "damned agnostics" in an angry mixture of Korean and English.

"Where's Hannah?" Jeannie asked, slyly. Carter knew that she had a good idea why Hannah was not with him in church that Sunday but her Vassar ring allowed her the benefit of the doubt when forsaking tact.

"Visiting her sister," Carter replied, offering just enough information to cut short further discussion on the subject.

"Then how about having dinner with us?"

"Tonight?"

"Unless you have other plans," said Jeannie, who probably figured that any evening plans Carter might have involved The Minnesota Vikings, TV, Schell ale, and him.

Carter considered the offer against the uncertain status of his marriage. "Sure," he said.

"Wonderful! Jeff loves company for Sunday dinner. He's a very good cook, you know. Is six o'clock too early?"

"No, that's fine. Can I bring something?"

"Just your appetite. We'll see you tonight?"

"You're on Fisher?"

"Yep, 153".

CHAPTER 2 ASK THE JEW

WHILE UNLOCKING THE DOOR to his office suite, Pastor Choi spotted Carter in the main hallway about to exit the church.

"Inspector Brand," he called out, "do you have a moment?"

Carter replied immediately, "Of course, *Moksanim*," and followed the pastor into his office suite. He took a seat on a couch in the reception area and waited for Choi to return from hanging his vestments in his office.

"Would you like some coffee, Carter?" Pastor Choi asked as Jeannie Park-Reed came into the room.

"I'm fine, *Moksanim*."

Seeing the impromptu meeting, Jeannie mouthed "Sorry," smiled at Carter, and discretely continued into the pastor's office. The pastor took a seat on an arm chair opposite Carter.

"I am not a wealthy man, Carter, and this matter should be trivial to someone with even the most basic financial skills. Keeping my personal accounts organized was my late wife's work and she did it very well, which left me free to concentrate on Gethsemane affairs. How can I put this...I need some help with filing my taxes this year."

Carter was puzzled. "Reverend, I would like to help you but I am a policeman. Don't you think it would be better to consult an accountant?"

"You're right, of course. That is just what people tell me. Please forgive my foolishness. I understood that your family was of the Jewish faith and as an officer of the law and a good church member I knew you would be someone I could trust."

Carter laughed politely. "Reverend Choi, it's a myth that all Jewish people are good with money. And even if that were true, my few tribal DNA threads barely qualified me to skip school during Passover when I was a boy."

"But, you must agree that God recognizes you and all the Jewish people as being special to Him, would you not agree?"

"I wouldn't know about that, Reverend. To me, people are mostly shaped by where they came from and what they experience in life as they get older."

"Ah, you say mostly, which tells me you can imagine other factors that determine who we become. I have so much respect for the Jewish people, Carter. They are a minority in this county, just as we Koreans are, yet they have attained positions of great influence in industry and politics. Doctors, lawyers, professors; everyone knows the best ones are Jewish because the best students are Jewish. I'm sure you have heard me preach on how we should strive to raise our children like the Jewish people raise theirs."

"I can tell you, *Moksanim*, I know many Jewish people who did not turn out how their parents would have liked."

"Exactly so. The Lord gave man free will. Look at what Joseph achieved in Egypt. Clearly, he was one anointed by God and Pharaoh recognized him as such. But look at what happened to the Kings of Israel. They sinned against the Lord and lost all that they had gained."

"I suppose. I see all kinds of people in my line of work. Many are desperate and commit crimes against society because they feel trapped and can't see any alternatives. Maybe the Israelites felt the same way."

"So, you see them as victims as much as sinners, then?"

"Oh, I don't know. I just arrest those who break the law and leave it to the courts to decide if they are guilty or not."

"You sound to me like you have much sympathy and compassion, Carter. You would make a good pastor."

Carter chuckled. "Sympathy for the devil perhaps, *Moksanim*."

"I noticed your wife was not with you this morning. Is she ill?"

"No, we just needed to have some time apart from each other, that's all."

Choi frowned. "Carter, I was married to my wife for forty-six years and I can't recall ever needing to be apart from her. Oh, there were times when I *wanted* to be apart from her but it was only - how might I say it - temporary insanity. How is it that you *needed* to be apart from her and she needed to be apart from you?"

From Reverend Choi, Carter did not consider the line of questioning intrusive. In fact, he would have been disappointed if the pastor had not asked. Had he been a more religious man Carter would have taken the matter up with Jesus, confessed his sinful nature, and felt cleansed through Christ's sacrifice. But faith that Jesus gave a rat's ass about him was an abstraction that he struggled with embracing on more than an intellectual level. He truly believed that Reverend Choi sincerely cared about him, cared about Hannah and cared about preserving their relationship.

"It's complicated. We need to discover what we really need in life," Carter said.

"Need or want?"

"In reality, aren't they both the same thing?"

"Perhaps in your reality, Carter, but not in mine and certainly not in God's. Do you love her?"

"Of course, I do."

"Then how could you say that you needed to be apart? You meant you wanted to be apart. While you are apart, just what is it that you hope to discover that might bring you closer with Hannah, or perhaps pull you farther apart still?"

"I wish I knew, Reverend. I really wish I knew."

"It is very important to me that you and Hannah work out your problems and remain married. That said, you must believe me when I tell you that your happiness is of equal importance. Try forgetting about yourselves for awhile and think about what you have together that you both care about deeply. And if you can't think of anything, think about what you might choose to care about. That's a question that I cannot help you with. You must bring that to the Lord."

CHAPTER 3 ETOUFFEE

CARTER ROLLED THE PRIUS up to 153 Fisher Avenue a few minutes before six. It was a cool, early November evening with dried autumn foliage swirling on the sidewalks. Jeannie and Jeff's home was a modest colonial that was in need of cosmetic attention not atypical of the parsonages of less distinguished pastors such as Jeffery Reed. Carter grabbed the brown paper packaged bottle of wine and started down the leaf-strewn walk. With each step, he considered what realistic expectations he might have for the evening.

He and Hannah tended to socialize with the married Korean church crowd where she could converse freely in her own tongue. This night, for the first time in five years, he would be alone and unclear about the status of his personal situation. He was not young, pushing fifty-two, but with his salt-and-pepper sideburns was still reasonably handsome and had maintained the physique nominally required of a senior police inspector.

Carter rang the doorbell and waited. After a long minute, he let drop the heavy brass doorknocker mounted just below the bell. Simultaneously, Jeannie Park-Reed

14

opened the front door and peeked around the side using the door as a vanity shield. She was wrapped in a towel; her hair still wet having just bolted from the shower. Pinching the towel corners together over her bosom, she let Carter in and scampered back to the bathroom.

"Why didn't you get the door?" she yelled to her husband as she ran past the kitchen.

"You know I can't leave a roux alone once it's started. It burns!" he shouted back.

Carter walked into the kitchen and found Jeff hunched over the stove, wooden spoon in hand, diligently stirring a cast iron skillet. Jeff was tall and thin with brown hair styled skillfully enough to mask the bald patch at the back of his head. His beard and mustache were well-groomed, consistent with his expertly tailored designer jeans and denim shirt. Carter parked the bag of wine on the counter and offered his hand in friendship.

"What's for dinner, Jeff?"

"Etouffee," he answered, presenting his unused hand for a shake as weak as church coffee. "I hope you're not allergic to shellfish," he sniffed.

"*Say-oo?*" Carter asked, hoping to impress with a pitiful attempt at Korean. Jeff continued stirring the thickening mixture.

"Shrimp?" Carter asked, this time in English.

"*Ga-jeh*" Jeannie corrected, entering the kitchen fully dressed but still fixing her hair. "Crawfish etouffee. We're eating Cajun tonight." Jeannie slid Carter's bottle of wine out of the bag and scanned the label. "Mmm, Russian River Valley - good choice!" Jeannie said, high-fiving Carter.

"Thanks, but I'm no connoisseur. The sign on the shelf in the liquor store said that *Wine Spectator* gave it 90 points so I figured how bad could it be?"

Five minutes after having brought the serving dishes to the table, Jeff's patience was gone. "Well, if we can tear away from this most *enlightening* conversation, dinner is served."

The round, oak dinner table was draped with a burgundy tablecloth, the overhang positioned equally around the perimeter. Unsure of the protocol, Carter paused momentarily to consider a seating arrangement of three people and a round table then arbitrarily chose a seat after realizing that it made no difference where he sat. Jeannie sat to his right.

"Let's pray," Jeannie requested with a touch of upspeak and grasped Carter's and Jeff's hands to her left and right. Carter bowed his head while Jeff offered grace.

"Heavenly father, we are forever surrounded by forces of darkness and evil who are committed to keeping us from your holy presence." Jeanie's grasp on Carter's hand tightened. Jeff continued. "Lord, thank you for allowing us this special time through your grace to share this magnificent food - and good wine - with our brother Carter. In your blessed name we pray, amen."

"Amen!" Jeannie agreed and Carter mumbled.

Jeff noticed the corked bottle of wine and frowned. "We can't drink this." he declared, clearly miffed. Carter was puzzled. Jeannie rolled her eyes.

"Hasn't properly breathed," Jeannie whispered to Carter who nodded discretely, suddenly aware of his cultural faux pas. Jeff grabbed the bottle by the neck and disappeared into the kitchen. Jeannie leaned closer to Carter and looking straight into his eyes asked, "Carter, are you a believer?"

At that moment Carter would have believed anything Jeannie Park-Reed told him. He had seen her dozens of times after services in church fellowship gatherings, but never one-on-one, close-up, alone. He sat mesmerized noticing every freckle, wrinkle and hair on her face with the subtle, skillful application of makeup perfectly emphasizing her exotic features. And the scent of perfumed soap radiating from her still-shower-warm body left him mute.

"I'm sorry," Carter said, snapping back to the conversation, "what was the question?"

"Are you a BELIEVER?" Jeannie repeated with a quick giggle at his distraction.

"I guess so, but my job requires I maintain a certain degree of skepticism about things."

Jeannie took Carter's hand firmly between hers and asked in a low voice, "Carter, do you believe Jesus died for you?"

"Yes," Carter answered in an equally low whisper, his eyes still locked on Jeannie's.

Jeff appeared with the wine and, for some reason, Carter did not worry about him seeing his gaze transfixed on his wife, nor did Jeannie. He poured a few ounces in a goblet, swirled it around the glass, tasted it and gave a grudging "hmph" of approval. After Jeff filled the three glasses with the now properly aerated Sauvignon Blanc, Jeannie toasted, "To our good friend Carter Brand who has honored us with his presence tonight."

Glasses clinked and the wine was drunk. During the dinner, Jeannie made sure Carter's glass was never empty.

CHAPTER 4 MONDAY NIGHT MURDER

DETRITUS OF CHINESE take-out food littered the glass-on-chrome coffee table. On the TV, the Minnesota Vikings were killing the last two minutes of a lopsided contest as the Blackberry's rudest ring shook Carter conscious:

FROM: MPLSSRV03

TO: INSP. BRAND

SUBJ: 10-54d

INVESTIGATE REPORT OF BODY W. LAKE ST. 11-98 KOBINSKI

Carter rubbed his eyes, stretched, grabbed keys to the Prius, tottered into the bathroom, peed, and left for the call.

It was 11:10 PM when he arrived at the crime site, pulling onto the wet grass that separated the shore of Lake Calhoun from a small, marshy patch of woods. Officer Kobinski was walking down a short path between the marsh and the road and met him at his car.

"Tree hugger!" Kobinski joked in mock derision at the sight of the Prius.

Carter opened the driver's side window. "What have we got?"

Kobinski read from his notepad: "White male, five foot-seven, about forty, no signs of a struggle. Strow is on the way."

Carter grabbed a digital camera and his case of investigative gear from the back seat and followed Kobinski up the path into the woods. The body lay face down in the grass fully dressed with a blood-soaked black sport jacket and khaki slacks. Carter began snapping pictures of the body from the top of its head to the soles of its shoes. After stretching into a pair of latex gloves from the "goody bag", he looked in the corpse's jacket pockets. He found nothing: no cell phone, no PDA, no items of any sort, electronic or otherwise. The same was true for the pants pockets - nothing.

Dr. Ostrow, coroner, arrived with two assistants in tow rolling a gurney over the soggy grass to the body. In one motion, they lifted it off the ground and placed it face up on the stretcher. Even in the dim moonlight Carter could recognize the muddied face of Dr. Kang.

Carter followed the gurney carting away the body down the path to the road. He shined his MagLite on the pavement where the path met the road and noted one large, muddy footprint which he reasoned was made by the killer just before stepping into a vehicle and driving away. He turned and retraced his steps to where the body was found, sweeping the path with the flashlight beam as he walked. Spots of blood reflected the light every few feet which told him that Kang was first shot or stabbed then dragged into the woods.

He got back into the Prius and slowly drove around the perimeter of Lake Calhoun looking for possible witnesses. Several hundred yards down the road, he passed two joggers. He pulled over to the side and opened the window as they passed.

"Excuse me," Carter said, badge in hand. The young women removed their iPod earbuds and came over to the car. "How long have you been jogging around Calhoun?"

One of the young women looked at her friend. "How long would you say, Sheila? About two years?" Sheila nodded.

"No, I meant tonight. How long have you been out here tonight?"

"Only about an hour, or so. Why?"

"We found a body in the woods down past the Recreation Center and we're looking for anyone who might have seen or heard anything in that area."

Sheila shook her head. "Oh, my goodness, no, we haven't seen anything. But I saw a guy fishing on the boat dock around there. He might still be there. You might ask him."

Carter circled back. By the side of the road about five hundred yards before the woods where Kang was found, he saw a man of about sixty stowing his fishing gear onto the bed of a pickup truck. He pulled up behind it.

"What are you catching?"

"Mostly a cold, don'tcha know. Got a few Muskies."

"How long have you been out here?"

"I'd say, about three hours...yah, three or four. Lookin' for someone, young fellah?"

Carter presented his badge. "There was a crime earlier this evening about a quarter mile down the road from here. Did you hear or see anything unusual?"

"Nope. Heard a bang echo across the lake around nine or ten, about when I got here, while I was takin' out my gear. But, yah, can't say that's real unusual around here. Kids are always chuckin' cherry bombs into the water. Don't know why. Scares the heck outta the fish, yah know? Then this SUV tears past like a bat outta hell. Nearly runs me over, for chrissake."

"Do you know what make or color it was?"

"Nah, it looked new."

"New how? Did it have those blue headlights or regular yellowish-white ones?"

"It was new. Yah, it just looked new."

CHAPTER 5 GIRL FRIDAY

JEANNIE PARK-REED had just collected the church mail when she entered Pastor Choi's office carrying two certified letters. "These are letters from Revelation Construction, *Moksanim*," Jeannie said and moved to deposit the envelopes on the pastor's desk. Choi peered over his glasses and waved her away.

"You open them Jeannie-*shi*," Choi said using the affectionate Korean diminutive. "You can bring me the translated copies later."

Jeannie scanned the documents into the office computer and proceeded to translate each one into *hangul* for the pastor and the elders. She laser printed two copies of each - one for the files and one for the pastor to review - and brought them to Choi's office.

"*Moksanim*, the letter says construction on the education center is being held up until we put two million dollars into the escrow account. Should I call Mr. Kwon?"

Choi frowned. "We can draw that down from our bank lines of credit, yes?"

"I think so, but shouldn't we check with Elder Kwon first?"

"No, no, let's not get too bureaucratic. Do it right away. I don't want to give them another excuse for more delays and Kang more ammunition to attack us with. We're already six months behind schedule."

"I can do this online. I have Mr. Kwon's authentication key."

"Good," Choi said, adjusting down his glasses and returning to his sermon preparation.

Much of Choi's administrative work was done by Jeannie Park-Reed. Two years ago, the church had posted an opening for a youth pastor on a Korean Methodist website anticipating the need to expand that ministry once the education center was built. Jeffery Reed responded and during the course of the interview it was discovered that his Korean wife had significant language and business skills which might allow the church to also fill the position previously handled by Choi's wife when she was alive. If there had been any question of Jeffery Reed's suitability for the Youth Pastor position those concerns were put to rest with the addition of Jeannie to the mix. He was offered the job.

Though Gethsemane was a well-funded, well-endowed church, their financial management was unsophisticated. Ledgers, journals, accounts and most other financial records were still in paper form when Jeannie and her husband arrived, with the weekly figures recorded in traditional "green-eyeshade" fashion.

Officially, Mr. Kwon, a retired South Korean C.P.A., was the elder in charge of church finances but everyone knew that Jeannie Park-Reed was the person to see for answers to most church finance questions. Within a year from the time she was hired, she had converted the church's hard-copy documents to electronic records processed with the latest business management software and replaced the ancient office machinery with a network of sleek computer workstations. With this new technology, the church was able to pay its bills, do more sophisticated financial forecasting and manage its banking online. These innovations proved invaluable for managing the complex financial details of the education center project, including pre-construction funding, milestone payments to contractors and optimizing the endowment fund's investment portfolio.

After two years at Gethsemane, Jeannie Park-Reed - now a church deacon - was regarded by most as the church's essential life force; the undisputable face of revitalization after the death of Pastor Choi's wife.

CHAPTER 6 HARDWOOD FLOOR

THE PROJECT MANAGER from the Revelation Construction Company, Tom DiGiorno, waited in the reception area outside Pastor Choi's office. He took a final slurp of coffee, wiped a few Styrofoam particles from his tongue and rose to greet his hosts.

"It's a pleasure to meet with you folks," he said with an embarrassingly exaggerated bow. "Thank you for agreeing to see me today. I know you all have more important things to deal with so I'll be..." Jeannie raised her hand to cut him off in order to allow her translation for the elders to catch up. She waved for him to continue. DiGiorno nodded acknowledging that he would have to pace his sales pitch with Jeannie's translation.

"We have a number of options for the gymnasium floor," said DiGiorno, "and I will explain the costs and benefits of each one. Please feel free to interrupt if you have any questions. We can just pour concrete and then paint on the sports patterns. That would be the cheapest option but it would be more expensive to heat. The next choice would be a hardwood floor like the better gyms, you know, like the pros use. It would be more expensive and would require more care and maintenance. The third option is a removable hardwood floor which gives you the best of both worlds, but it is the most expensive."

"How much more expensive is the removable floor than the hardwood?" Elder Kwon asked in Korean for the benefit of his fellow elders. Jeannie translated for DiGiorno.

"About fifty-percent," DiGiorno replied.

"Would you please give us a few minutes to discuss the matter?" Choi asked in English.

"No problem, take all the time you need," said DiGiorno, holding up a cigarette in front of Jeannie and raising his eyebrows to request permission. She shook her head no.

"We would like to select the hardwood floor," said Choi. "How soon can we have it installed?"

"What's your timeframe?"

"As soon as possible. We can't have any more delays."

"We can have it by the end of the month. Does that fit your schedule?"

"That would be fine."

DiGiorno rose to leave, shaking the elders' hands as they filed past him. "I will need a deposit today if we are to meet that delivery date, though," DiGiorno said as he put on his coat, an unlit cigarette dangling from his lips.

"How much?" Jeannie asked.

"Let me check." DiGiorno opened his briefcase and danced his fingers over his calculator keys. "Twenty. Can you handle it?"

"Jeannie," said Choi, "write Mr. DiGiorno a check from the gymnasium budget."

Jeannie had contingency checks that Elder Kwon had signed in advance and made one out for twenty-thousand dollars. DiGiorno accepted it, put it in his briefcase and handed her a receipt.

CHAPTER 7 LIKELY SUSPECTS

THOUGH CARTER WAS the senior inspector in the homicide division, he decided to enlist the assistance of a young Korean detective from fraud investigations for the Kang case. It wasn't so much that he was suspecting financial malfeasance at that point, but since the victim was Korean there was a good likelihood that the investigation would require a knowledge of Korean language and culture that Carter did not posses. Jae-Sun "Jason" Kim was also known to have the superior computer skills that Carter lacked.

Carter sat at his desk staring at his computer's wallpaper photo of Hannah he had taken a few months before they were married. It was summer and they had just playfully soaked each other with a garden hose. She was beaming, menacingly pointing the nozzle in his direction; sunglasses rotated over the top of her head. The folder Jason plopped on Carter's desk snapped him to the present.

"Here are the first database searches on Sangwoo Kang, boss."

Carter stretched in his swivel chair. "What've we got?"

"We searched Metropolitan and FBI - haven't yet gone through his medical records. He was a cosmetic surgeon, did you know that?"

"Yeah, he started coming to Gethsemane a few years after we did. I never saw him with a woman so I figured he was unmarried."

"Well, Last year he was sued for malpractice by one Tiffani Johnson for a botched boob job. He won the case."

"She wasn't an easy loser I assume?"

"Correct. He was granted a restraining order on her after she pulled some seriously ungracious shit: threatening phone calls to his home, office and cell, bogus subscriptions to kiddie porn websites, slashing his tires, you know the usual."

"Ok, she qualifies. Let's pay her a visit. What else?"

Jason drew out another sheet from the folder. "His nurse, or medical assistant as she's referred to in the deposition, a Jessica Ahn, sued him, also last year, for sexual harassment. It was settled out-of-court with the terms not listed."

"That's it?"

"Not quite. It seems Ms. Ahn's boyfriend, a Donald Benezek decided a financial settlement wasn't good enough and felt the need to defend his lady's virtue personally. Kang filed complaints against him for violent threats left on his answering machine."

Carter grabbed his coat off the chair back. "Let's start with our distressed breasts lady."

Jason checked the sheet. "She's in Kenwood."

"I'll drive," Carter said.

CHAPTER 8   IT FIGURES

THE RED BRICK garden apartment building was attractive, but it still looked out of place in the neighborhood of modern, upscale houses. At the door, Carter turned to Jason. "Now be professional and promise me you won't stare at her chest, OK?"

The doorbell sounded three musical "dings" which Carter recognized as the first notes of a once popular song the exact title of which escaped him at that moment.

"Just a minute," screeched a voice from inside the apartment. Tiffani Johnson opened the door greeting them both with an ear-to-ear smile; a scary, Baby Jane smile. She had to have been seventy, if she was a day, with tightly permed blond hair, large hoop earrings and makeup applied with enough excess to mask the aging features of her probably-once-pretty face. She wore tight designer jeans and a loose fitting "St. Paul is for Lovers" T-shirt with the tails knotted together under a prodigious bust line. Jason's gaze was instinctively drawn to her breasts which, to his youthful estimation, showed no evidence of disfiguration.

"Please, come in and make yourselves comfortable," she beckoned, and led them to a borscht-red velvet couch.

She took a position on a loveseat across the coffee table and curled her legs beneath her. "Can I get you something to drink? Coffee?" she asked through stained, capped teeth.

Sensing things might get stranger, Carter got straight to the point. "We're investigating the murder of Doctor Sangwoo Kang..."

"Yes, I read about it in the paper. Terrible. And you think because of what he did to me I would hold a big grudge to kill him?"

"We're just following up with anyone who has had a conflict with him in the past, ma'am."

"Well, it wasn't me, but you could hardly blame me if I did it after what that butcher did to me. Here, let me show you. You be the judge if he didn't get just what he deserved."

Carter stopped her short as she began to unknot her tee-shirt's tails. "That won't be necessary, ma'am. We just want to know where you were last Friday night around ten PM."

"My, aren't WE getting personal. Where were YOU last Friday at ten o'clock?" the lady said through a fossilized grin.

Raising an eyebrow, Carter shot one of those icy "don't-fuck-with-me-lady" stares that better detectives develop after years of challenging interviews.

"OK, I was with my lover, Tyler," she answered, coyly.

Carter was dubious. Jason looked reflexively at the boobs. "We need to have Tyler verify that. Can you give us his address?" Carter slid a notepad and pen across the coffee table. She slid the notepad back.

"He lives here."

"Is he here now?"

31

Tiffani shook a Virginia Slims out of a tortoise shell cigarette case, tamped it three times, lit it, took a deep drag and exhaled. "He's out buying cigarettes,"

"We'll wait for Tyler here, if that's alright with you."

"Suit yourself," she said and took another drag.

Five minutes passed before Tiffani crushed out her cigarette in a souvenir ashtray from a lesser known Vegas casino. Carter and Jason turned towards the sound of jangling keys. Through the front door walked a man they presumed to be Tyler.

After years of professionally entering the lives of all manner of humanity, Carter thought he was able to remain unfazed from even the most bizarre domestic situation. But seeing Tyler made him wince. Here was a painful caricature of an aging gigolo with ripped Texas boots and long, greasy, dyed-blond hair cut in a style briefly popular twenty-five years earlier. He leaned over the sofa and deposited a carton of Virginia Slims next to Tiffani. She drew him to her face by the collar and gave him a long, passionate, wet kiss.

"Thanks, lover," she cooed.

Carter fought to hide his revulsion. Jason grimaced. Carter stood to shake Tyler's hand. Tyler disdainfully scanned him from head to toe.

"Who are you?" he asked, smugly.

Carter put his badge in Tyler's face with his left hand and shook Tyler's clammy, limp hand with his right. "Inspector Brand with Minneapolis Police, sir." Tiffani pulled from her lips one of the two cigarettes she had lit and passed it to Tyler. Carter pointed to Jason. "This is Sgt. Kim."

Tiffani glanced at Jason. "Kim? Are you related to Betty Kim? She does my nails. She's Korean, you know." Jason did not respond. Carter continued.

"We've been speaking with Ms. Johnson about her whereabouts last Friday at ten o'clock. She claims she was with you. Can you corroborate that?"

Carter sensed from Tyler's vacant stare that his mental clutch plate was starting to slip. Tiffani came to his rescue.

"He means do you agree, angel,"

"Yeah, ten o'clock." Tyler smirked.

"AM or PM? Morning or night?" Jason tagged in with a dangerous "wipe-that-grin-off-your-face" tone.

"Both!" Tyler chortled, through black and yellow-stained teeth, clearly pleased with his remarkably snappy retort. Tiffani puckered her smeared lips and blew him a kiss.

Into the room walked a slight man of about seventy or eighty wearing jeans and a heavy parka, balancing three full brown paper grocery sacks in his arms. "Cupcake, they were out of Diet Pepsi so I had to buy Diet Coke. That's OK, right? I can bring it back if you don't want. I got the Bacardi." He eyeballed Carter. "Who are you?"

Carter and Jason produced their badges. "We are Minneapolis police detectives investigating a homicide. And you are..?" Carter asked.

The man looked at Tiffani for permission to respond. She shrugged. "Perry. Perry Johnson. This is my house. We don't know nothin' about no murder."

"He's my husband. He don't know nothin' about nothin'," Tiffani scowled.

Carter stood and gestured to Jason that it was time to split. Tiffani smiled and offered her hand for him to kiss. He shook it loosely. "Thank you Ms. Johnson..."

"Please, MRS. Johnson. I am a married woman, you know," she said with girlish indignation.

Carter turned for the door with Jason close behind. "We'll be in touch if we have any further questions. Thank you for your time."

In the Prius, Carter put the key in the ignition and paused. "Can you tell me what that was all about?"

Jason shook his head. "Beats me, but I really need to go home and hug my kid!"

CHAPTER 9 GAME

BACK AT HIS DESK, Carter struggled to concentrate on the Johnson interview. As bizarre as it was, there was still the possibility that one or more of those characters were involved in Kang's demise and he needed to sort it out before moving on.

But Jeannie Park-Reed dominated his thoughts. Like digital photobursts, he flashed on every encounter with her since leaving Hannah at the airport, each one more inspiriting than the last. Right then he wanted nothing more than to be close to her, for any reason, just to look into her soft, brown eyes and to hear her angelic voice saying anything.

Carter was still a Christian man and knew that even a quasi-religious man like he should stay on the good side of the Ten Commandments. He clicked on *dictionary.com* to remind him of - if he ever really knew - the meaning of the verb "to covet" and parsed the definition until he was comfortable that he was still on the "shalt not" side.

Text message on the Blackberry:

From: jpr@gethkumc.org

WHAT DO YOU LIKE ON YOUR PIZZA? 8:00

35

TONIGHT MY PLACE. JPR

He pressed REPLY on the Blackberry and tapped in

ANCHOVIES <SEND>.

He could not remember ever ordering anchovies on his pizza but it seemed less plain than sausage or mushrooms and impressing Jeannie Park-Reed became a priority at that moment.

It was drizzling lightly as Carter arrived precisely at eight o'clock, simultaneous with the pizza delivery boy. Jeannie opened the door in sweatpants and damp Vassar track jersey, the shelf of her bosom standing spruce. Carter paid for the pizza and carried it inside.

"I was about to go jogging but it got too rainy. Wanna beer?"

Carter thought for a moment and decided that accepting a beer from a good Christian woman would not lower his standing in her or God's eyes. "Sure," he said.

Jeannie sat two tall bottles of an obscure German pilsner in front of Carter and returned to the kitchen. He grabbed a bottle, twisted the cap and immediately realized that this mysterious brand was probably from the last bottler on earth who still sealed their brew with non-twist-off caps. He put the bottle down carefully to avoid looking to Jeannie like a complete moron.

Jeannie returned with two frosty beer steins and a bottle opener. "We're going to need a church key to open these bottles. Jeff likes this brand of beer. It's from Frankfurt, I think. He's a purist; believes if it has a twist-off bottle cap it can't be any good." She popped the caps and filled both steins simultaneously, the foamy heads settling down equally to a perfect height. Carter was impressed.

"Very professional, Jeannie."

"I tended bar part-time while at Vassar. Some tricks you never forget. Did you know that Germany has a law that controls what can and cannot be put in beer?"

"I think I heard of it," Carter said, not wanting to appear shallow, and took a gulp from the mug.

"It was called *Reinheitsgebot* and it said that beer could only be made from water, barley and hops. It figures, right? While other nations were arguing over what moral and ethical laws to pass for the good of their people the Germans were mostly concerned about not screwing up the beer."

Carter guffawed, catching himself before jetting beer through his nostrils. She was brilliant, beautiful and funny. "You worked in a bar? Somehow I don't see a Vassar girl slinging beer."

Jeannie laughed. "Why not? Did you know Vassar College was founded on beer money? Matt Vassar was the country's most successful brewer at one point."

Carter opened the pizza box. Cheese was stuck to the cover and hung down like gooey stalactites.

Jeannie slammed the box closed. "This is the last time I order pizza from Sabrina's! I know they have those little plastic stands to keep the cheese from sticking to the box, goddamn cheap-ass dagos!" This was not the behavior of the sweet JPR that he had come to know. In fact, it was a bit frightening.

"Jeannie, it's fine. When I was a kid we never had plastic pizza box tripods. We always thought the cardboard flavor was just part of how pizza was supposed to taste."

Her contemptuous expression softened and the sweet smile Carter remembered returned with her composure. "Sorry," she said sheepishly. "Let's pray: Lord, we thank you for food we are about to receive. Amen," she raced. She beamed. "Carter, I have a present for you," she said and handed him a neatly wrapped rectangular gift box.

It caught Carter by surprise. "For me?" he asked, and playfully lifted and lowered it to gauge its weight. "Hmm...too heavy for a necktie."

"C'mon. Open it!" Jeannie begged with child-like anticipation.

Carter carefully removed the wrapping paper and opened the box. Inside he found a leather-bound copy of the King James Bible. "Wow, and I haven't even finished Christianity for Dummies."

"I like the King James even with its archaic English. It just seems more authentic when I read words like 'oblations' instead of 'offerings'. Much more literate, don't you think?"

"I suppose, but I'm not nearly as well-read as you are. I'll need a dictionary when I find words like oblation."

After they finished the pizza Jeannie daintily licked spots of sauce from her fingers and dabbed her lips clean with a napkin. With the same napkin, she wiped sauce off Carter's chin. He smiled. "Thanks, mom."

"Carter, do you play backgammon?"

"I used to in college, but that was a long time ago. I played for money with the betting cube. Won enough money to pay for my books but I don't think I would even be able to setup a game now."

Jeannie reached over to the bookshelf, grabbed an elegant, leather attaché case backgammon set and opened it on the table in front of Carter and herself. "I'll get us started. You just throw the dice and remember which direction you're going," Jeannie said and tossed the red and white pieces perfectly into place. She assigned Carter the white checkers.

They threw one die each to begin the game.

Each threw a six.

They threw again.

Each threw a four.

On the third throw, Jeannie tossed a one, Carter a two.

Jeannie was amused. "It's looking like we're going to be playing for awhile," she said. Carter inched forward his pieces on Jeannie's home board. "Pretty conservative," she taunted.

"I'm a pretty cautious guy," Carter countered. Jeannie threw a four and five and nailed both of Carter's exposed pieces. She smiled devilishly. He raised his eyebrows. "And you're pretty reckless."

"No risk-no reward, nothing ventured-nothing gained, blah, blah, blah."

Carter looked puzzled. "Why would you risk sending your advanced pieces back to the beginning just to put my less valuable ones back just a few points?"

"I have faith in the Lord," she declared with a smile, rolling her eyes skyward. Carter wasn't sure why the creator of heaven and earth would be concerned with protecting Jeannie's ill-advised backgammon moves but there was much about The Faith that he assumed Jeannie understood much better than he.

He threw the dice. One and four, liberating both of his jailed pieces and sending one of Jeannie's back to the beginning. Carter cocked his head in an I-told-you-so gesture.

Jeannie remained unruffled. "Game's far from over, darling," she said and threw double fours sending her piece out of captivity and out of danger and covering one of her exposed pieces in the process.

The parry and thrust continued for about an hour with each sticking to their original strategies until Jeannie had four pieces left on the number six point on her home board and Carter had four on his number one. It was his turn.

Carter looked up at Jeannie. "Well, my dear, it looks like we've reached the moment of truth. If I throw any double I win. But even If I don't, you still must throw a double six, and only a double six, to win." Carter threw three and four and took two of his four remaining pieces off the board.

She locked her eyes onto his, picked up the dice and tossed them. Double six.

Jeannie's eyes stayed glued to his as if she knew the outcome could never have been otherwise. Carter considered the odds but was comfortable with the notion that luck had nothing to do with it. She was wired to a higher power against which he stood no chance.

Carter stood up and stretched extending a hand of congratulations to Jeannie. "Whew, that was intense. Where's Jeff?"

"Oh, he has youth Bible study tonight and they often stay late."

"Well, say hello for me. Gotta scoot - early meeting tomorrow."

"How is the case coming?" Jeannie asked while helping Carter into his coat.

"Moving along.. Still have a number of witnesses to talk to and suspects to check out."

"It's all just terrible. Everyone is so horrified," Jeannie shivered. She put her arms around him and held him tightly, resting her head on his shoulder. "And scared."

Carter instinctively pinned his arms to his side then slowly raised them around her and held her tightly in return. He wanted nothing more than to kiss her but did not dare - not even a European cheek-peck.

"Good night," he whispered and left.

CHAPTER 10 FEATHERWEIGHT

SEEING CARTER'S coffee-stained desk blotter, Jason placed the foam cup just out of arm's reach. "Cream, no sugar, right?" Carter verified, without diverting his attention from the newspaper.

"10-4, extra cholesterol. You're never going to believe what I discovered on the web about our lovebirds."

"Try me."

"I Googled PERRY JOHNSON and found a bunch of old articles in the Trib's archives. About fifty years ago, Mr. Johnson was a contending featherweight, 12-0 with eight knockouts at one point. He and his stripper girlfriend were real tabloid darlings. Guess what the stripper's name was?"

"Candy? Bambi?" Carter guessed, with his concentration remaining fixed on his newspaper.

"Tiffani, with an 'I'," Jason said, clearly excited about his chance discovery. Carter put down his newspaper and coffee and reached over to examine Jason's report. Jason pulled it back. "But wait, there's more!" Carter twisted his glasses up.

Jason flipped through the printout. "OK, here it is. I found this in the gossip column. The Johnsons were regulars at a few of the downtown saloons, but one of them, Corky's, was Perry's castle. He was also an owner in the place - it didn't say how deep. Anyway, one night Hawthorn Hayden walks in. He was a fighter, black, who had handed Perry his first defeat a few months before. That night, Perry and Tiffani had a very big, very public fight at Corky's, which resulted in a shiner on her and some facial damage to him.

Meanwhile, Hayden's been holding court at a bar stool slowly driving Perry nuts. For revenge, apparently, Tiffani sidles up to Hayden and gets cozy. This is too much for Perry who unloads on Hayden's head with a long-neck beer bottle beating him nearly to death. He's arrested and serves a year at Shakopee. He was only sentenced to six months but wasn't exactly a model prisoner. I found that out by cross-referencing the newspaper dates with our old arrest records."

Carter returned his attention to the newspaper and coffee. "Interesting story, but how do you tie that to the late Dr. Kang?"

"Here's what I'm thinking. I'm no psychologist, but maybe, just maybe, Perry flashed back to his macho glory days to break his cuckold status defending Tiffani's honor by killing Kang."

"Cuckold?"

"Yeah, it means pussy-whipped husband."

"I think you cooked up this whole theory just so you could use 'cuckold' in a sentence."

"Hey, I was a liberal arts major at school, so sue me."

Carter scrunched an incredulous frown. "Honor? Tiffani? Isn't that a contradiction in terms?"

"Maybe but remember how much he adored her and what a pitiful shadow of his former self he is now. He might have killed Kang just to raise his own self esteem."

Carter was still unconvinced. "Let's keep that theory in our back pocket, shall we, and visit the harassed Ms. Ahn and her chivalrous beau."

CHAPTER 11 COP TIME

PARKED BEHIND a late model Toyota Corolla in Jessica Ahn's driveway sat a '70s-vintage Pontiac GTO striped with body primer ready for a long overdue paint job. Jason pulled-up the unmarked olive-green Fairlane in front of a single-story bungalow at the end of a cul-de-sac off Como.

A couple standing on the porch steps spotted Carter and Jason approaching. They scrambled back into the house and slammed the door shut.

"Back door!" Carter shouted. Jason sprinted left to the backyard, Carter trotted right. "Police! Stop!" Carter commanded, badge waving. In the backyard, Jason caught up to a Goth-attired, bespectacled young man and pulled him down by his belt as he attempted to scale a shoulder-high wooden fence. They rolled in the grass. The man sprang to his feet and started to flee. Jason grabbed him. The man threw a clumsy punch grazing Jason's shoulder. Carter grabbed him from behind and struggled to slap on handcuffs. He whirled and bit Carter's hand. "Goddammit," Carter screamed and snapped his hand back to examine the damage. Jason wrestled the man to the ground, sat on him and cuffed him.

45

The man's girlfriend charged out the backdoor wearing just a size XXL Vikings jersey and dove at Jason, screaming curses in Korean. The jersey flew up to her waist as Jason deftly tossed her aside. She was not a natural blond.

Carter, panting, cuffed her and read both of them Miranda rights in English. Jason repeated in Korean then called for a car to transport the couple back to the precinct.

At the station, Jessica Ahn and Donald Benezek were moved to separate interrogation rooms. Carter began with Benezek. He was sitting on a metal chair in room I-3, uncuffed. His scraggy beard and mustache were unkempt, as was his greasy ponytail, partially obscured by the hood of his grimy army surplus parka.

Carter began the interrogation. "Donald, what do you like to be called? Donny? Don?"

Benezek shrugged, "Don is good."

"Don, can I bring you some coffee, a Coke?"

"Can I get a Mountain Dew?"

"Of course, Don." Carter gestured for a detective to bring the drink. He put on his glasses and perused Benezek's rap sheet. "You've built quite a record, Don: Passing bad checks, selling phony prescriptions, public indecency." Carter glanced at Benezek over the top of his glasses. "Public indecency?"

"I peed in the street and this old lady took offense."

Carter removed and folded his glasses. "Donald, you know we're not here to talk about flashing an old lady. You're in quite a bit of trouble. We found a dozen vials of schedule 5 pharmaceuticals in your girlfriend's house, Oxycontin, Ritalin, Dexedrine. The labels indicate they were all prescribed by S. Kang, Jessica's Boss." Benezek shrugged. "Care to explain how the drugs came into your possession?"

The part of love's unwritten covenant that includes loyalty must have escaped Benezek. "They're Jessica's. She made the doctor give her the 'scripts. I told her we would get busted but she did it anyway. I drive a cab so I don't make much money - maybe three hun'ert on a good week - and she wants expensive shit like three hun'ert dollar haircuts. I said, 'baby, it ain't worth it, we have each other, right? We'll get bye' ."

"Stop, Donald, or you're going to make me cry. And you bolted this morning because you didn't want to be found with Jessica's drugs, right?"

"Well, yeah, no point in both of us getting busted."

"I'm so glad we had this conversation, Don. I would never have guessed what a romantic young man you are - and so wise."

Benezek rose from his seat to leave. "So, I guess I can go, right?"

"Stay put, young man. We have a lot more to talk about." Carter turned to leave the room shaking his head. "Maybe when we continue our conversation you can give me some pointers on achieving a successful relationship."

Jason was waiting for Carter in room I-2. Jessica, in the same Vikings jersey, now tucked in her jeans, was sipping Diet Coke through pasty fluorescent lipstick, marking time, eyes fixed straight ahead.

Jason briefed him. "She's not being very cooperative, boss. She worked for Kang so she must speak some English but she only responds to Korean." Jessica rotated her chair 180 degrees turning her back on her interrogators.

"OK, you translate, but frankly, I don't even know why we're here. We got the whole story from Donny: Jessica wanted a bigger crib, newer car and brought home pills she forced Donald to sell for her. Case closed."

Jessica spun the chair around, sending her can of Coke flying across the room. With eyes blazing with fury, she was ready to burst, but caught herself before betraying her English fluency. Jason translated the essence of Carter's provocation into Korean. Immediately, she barked back her response, also in Korean. Jason translated, matching her tone as she continued to rant.

"She says she's innocent and I think the closest I can translate her description of him might be *limp-dick sodomite.*"

"When she calms down let's hear her side of the story."

Carter hoped to hear anything that might slip to indicate complicity with the death of Kang. It was obvious to him that either Kang had attempted to solicit sex from her by supplying her with narcotics or that she had seduced him with the promise of sexual favors in return for drugs. In either case, silencing a partner in crime was emerging as a strong motive.

Jessica ended her tirade and sat fuming with folded arms. Then she broke and shouted in clear English, "I want a lawyer! I mean it. I want a lawyer now!"

CHAPTER 12 JESSICA TALKS

IF ONE OF the partners-in-crime was the brains-of-the-outfit it certainly was not the dimwitted Donald Benezek. So, it didn't surprise Carter that Jessica had called a private attorney rather than requesting a public defender. She sat in a conference room with her lawyer, Philip Kim, discussing her options in Korean.

Carter and Jason waited outside the door watching them through the window. "What do you think?" Jason asked.

"I think she was clever enough to know that we were looking for her boss's killer and not just small-time pill pushers. I'm sure he's counseling her to cop a plea for just the drugs in return for immunity from any future charges that might be related to Kang's murder."

Assistant District Attorney Grace Campion arrived to take charge of the Ahn-Benezek case. "Nearly froze my tits off out there," she said, rapidly rubbing together her deerskin-gloved hands. It was a typical Grace Campion entrance, designed for maximum shock value immediately putting both colleagues and opponents on the defensive.

"Let me get you some coffee, ma'am," Jason said.

"Thanks, um?"

"Jason. Jason Kim."

"Thank you, Jason. Black with two Equals, please." She unbuttoned her full-length sable coat and peeked through the window. "Forgive me for asking the obvious, but she was Mirandized, I assume?"

Carter confirmed. "Yes. She stayed mostly silent and gave up nothing of any significance. Her boyfriend, however, was more than willing to have her take the rap for the pills."

"Would she be willing to testify against him?"

"I would guess. There doesn't appear to be much love lost between them right now."

Campion glanced over the case documents. "They're not married so spousal privilege won't be an issue. I'm going for illegal possession of controlled substances with intent to distribute, Brand. Any problem with that?"

"Actually, Grace, I'm more interested in tying them to the Kang murder. They had a beef with him last year and there's evidence that Kang supplied the pills that these two peddled. I'm thinking that something went wrong in that arrangement and the doctor ended up dead. The way they panicked when we showed up at their pad reinforces my suspicion."

Jason returned with her coffee. She took a sip and smiled.

"Pad? C'mon, Carter, you're showing your age now. We say 'crib' these days."

"Right, forgive my acid flashback."

"Let's see what she's willing to give up and what he wants in return. If there's not much of any use we'll go for the drugs and move on, deal?"

Carter had little interest in busting petty drug dealers. His job was to capture killers and he needed to make sure each possibility, no matter how unlikely, was thoroughly explored before moving on to the next. ADA Campion, the presumptive Democratic candidate for District Attorney, wanted convictions. The more the better.

Through the window, Attorney Kim motioned for the group to come into the room. "They're done," Campion said, and assigned her half-empty coffee cup to Jason for disposal. She marched into the room ahead of Carter and Jason where they took seats at the table opposite Kim and Ahn.

The lawyer rose to shake Campion's hand.

"Good to see you again, Grace."

"Philip," she responded.

"My client is willing to cooperate fully with your investigation provided she has assurances that you will respect a scope that would protect her rights against self incrimination. Can we start there?"

Campion dismissed the offer with a smirk. "Don't diddle me, Kim. I don't play on that team. We have all the evidence we need to send both of these clowns away for a long time. I can't imagine what you might have that I would have the remotest interest in."

"Oh, I think you and the Inspector have a very good idea what Miss Ahn might provide. If your case against her was all that airtight we would not be sitting here chatting, now would we?"

Campion stood up to leave. "This is Minnesota, Counselor. I could walk into the courtroom and get first degree drug with aggravation before my nails dried."

Attorney Kim reached out for her to stay. "OK, third degree and we allow broader questioning about Kang."

"Second degree and she agrees to testify against Benezek."

"Second with no aggravation," the lawyer stipulated. "And no jail time."

Campion sat down. "I'll make my recommendation to the judge based on the value of her testimony."

"So we have a deal? Third degree?"

"Second with no aggravation. You have the floor Inspector," Campion said and passed the questioning to Carter.

He looked up from his notes. "Miss Ahn, how were you able to get Dr. Kang to provide you with prescriptions for the narcotics?"

She looked at her attorney for permission to respond. He nodded. She continued.

"You know, Donald told me to steal prescription blanks from the doctor's office. You know, like I would forge Kang's signature and his writing. Donald showed me what to write, you know?"

"You were able to buy this quantity of controlled drugs without arousing suspicions?"

"You know, I would go to the busy pharmacies. Like the pharmacists were too busy to look at the 'scripts too close, you know? One time a pharmacist called Kang to see if the 'script was good and he said, like, OK, it's OK."

"I don't understand. Kang told the pharmacist the prescription was good?"

"Yeah, so I go to work the next day and he doesn't say nothin' about it until I got my coat on to go home at night then he says he wants me to come over his place that night. I say I don't have time and then he goes, like, he knows about the 'scripts and if I don't come over he'll call the cops so I go over." Jessica looked over to her lawyer for a sign that she had related enough information to fulfill the agreement.

"Tell them what happened at Kang's place, Jessica."

"He said I should come home with him after work each day. He would have Korean food delivered or sometimes, take-out, you know, like I was his girlfriend or something. So, like, I would go over and when I went to leave he asks me what kind of 'script I wanted and he would give it to me if I had sex with him and I would take it home and got it filled and Donald sold the pills mostly to college kids. Mostly speed, you know?"

"Did Donald know what you were doing to get the prescriptions?" Carter asked.

"Well, yeah, duh. He wanted me to go over more, like on the weekends and holidays so he could get more 'scripts."

Carter looked over the research Jason had collected on Kang. "Tell me about the sexual harassment suit."

"One day, the doctor doesn't want me to go over anymore. He gets all religious and tells me Father God led his girlfriend back to him and he doesn't want me to come over no more. Real creepy, you know?"

"And I assume that was the end of the 'scripts as well?"

"Yeah, and Donald was real fuckin' pissed off. He sold all these college kids pills and now he had to give the money back. He knew if he sued Kang for sexual harassment he could get a lot of money 'cause Kang wouldn't want anyone to know about us and the 'scripts."

"So, if Kang settled, why did Donald threaten him?"

"He just wanted more pills, you know? He wanted to pimp me back to Kang for more 'scripts, *gaeseki*! But Kang didn't care about me no more. He went to church all the time and started begging me to forgive him. He goes, 'Jessica, it's not too late for you to be saved by the blood of Christ'. *Really* creepy. Donald told Kang that he would kill him if he didn't give me more 'scripts."

Campion put down her Blackberry she had been texting into. "He said that? He said he would kill Kang?"

The lawyer put his hand in front of his client's mouth to stop her from answering. "I think we're finished for today, gentlemen. Grace, I'll see you tomorrow in your office? I'm sure you want this wrapped up as soon as possible. We can work out the details."

Carter wanted to move forward with his case as well but not in the direction ADA Campion had it heading. She had a solid drug case against Benezek but Jessica dropping that quote that he intended to kill Kang sounded pretty fishy to him - like something her lawyer came up with to draw attention away from his client. How much of the story was real and how much was fabrication constructed by a very clever attorney who knew what words might satisfy the agendas of all parties sitting across the table, Carter did not know. Nonetheless, it was all he had to go on.

CHAPTER 13 LIGHTLY BEATEN

WITH COOKWARE and carefully measured ingredients strategically laid out on the kitchen counter, Carter prepared for final assembly of his evening's dinner. The doorbell squawked. Disconcerted, he placed the egg back in its carton, stepped into the living room, lowered the music and pressed the intercom button. The image of the visitor at the lobby door snapped onto the video screen. It was Jeannie Park-Reed.

"Jeannie?"

"Carter, it's me. I hope you don't mind me stopping by without calling ahead."

"No, it's fine. C'mon up," he said, and buzzed her in. He grabbed the dirty socks off the sofa, tossed them into his bedroom and did a quick scan of the apartment for anything else that should not be seen by a classy female guest. Moments later, Jeannie knocked a "shave-and-a-haircut" beat on the condo door. Carter ran his fingers over his hair and let her in.

"Jeannie, what a pleasant surprise."

"I found your address in the church membership records. You're not mad, are you?"

"Of course not, come on in."

"You left the Bible I bought you at my place the other day. I was in the neighborhood so I thought I'd bring it by," she said, handing Carter the leather-bound book.

"Oh, thanks, I had so much on my mind that night."

Jeannie noticed the array of recipe components through the kitchen doorway. "I'm sorry, I see I interrupted your dinner."

"No, no, that's fine. I had just started making it. Would you like to stay and have dinner with me?" Carter asked, hopefully.

"Thanks, no. I should be going."

"Please stay," Carter appealed, gently. "You must let me reciprocate for dinner at your house last week, though it won't be anywhere near as fancy."

She paused to consider the request. "What are you making?"

Carter led Jeannie into the kitchen. "Well, once again I'm trying my hand at making authentic matzo ball soup but I can never get it quite right. They always come out either too rubbery or too loose."

"Let me see how you're doing it. Maybe I can help."

"You have experience making matzo balls?" Carter asked, even though he had come to believe that there was nothing beyond Jeannie Park-Reed's capabilities.

She washed her hands in the kitchen sink and shook them dry. "I had a roommate at Vassar who invited me to her home on Long Island one year for Passover. I watched how her mom made the matzo balls. Let me see how you do it," she said, standing behind him, her hand affectionately on his shoulder.

"OK, I have everything ready for assembly. First I mix the matzo meal, oil and salt. Then I add..." Jeannie intercepted Carter's hand before it struck an egg against the mixing bowl rim.

"You weren't going to drop that egg in the meal just like that, were you?"

"I was going to crack it open first, if that's what you mean."

"No, I meant you weren't going to beat the eggs beforehand?"

"No, I wasn't planning to. Should I?"

"Well, I think I've found your problem then. If you beat the eggs lightly before you mix them in with the dry ingredients the balls will be easier to roll and they'll come out fluffy, not bouncy, if you cook them properly. Also, try mixing in about an eighth of a teaspoon of baking soda with the water and you can forget the seltzer."

"No seltzer? Oy, my grandmother is turning over in her grave."

"I'll bet, and from a *shiksa*, no less," she laughed.

Carter reached above the counter and grabbed a cereal bowl for the eggs. "Don't have another mixing bowl and I think the only baking soda I've got is an open box in the refrigerator to absorb odors."

"Any port in a storm. Maybe it will give the matzo balls an interesting flavor," Jeannie said optimistically and with just her left hand cracked open each egg into the bowl. Carter whisked the eggs with a fork before stirring them into the matzo meal with the remaining ingredients.

"We have, what, fifteen minutes before we can roll the balls?" Carter asked on his way to the living room. "Care for some wine?"

"Thirty is better, and, yes, I would love some."

"It's in the fridge."

Jeannie opened the refrigerator door and located a free space on the top shelf for the bowl of matzo meal to let the mixture rest. She did a quick inventory of the refrigerator's contents: a bottle of wine, milk, ketchup, beer, a few paper containers of Chinese take-out leftovers and a Tupperware jar of aging kimchi. "I assume you're keeping the kimchi for sentimental reasons?"

Carter stepped back into the kitchen. "Not funny," he said, and closed the refrigerator door.

"Sorry, that was insensitive of me."

"Forget it. Let's open that wine. There's a corkscrew in the drawer."

Jeannie found two wine goblets and wiped them clean with a moistened paper towel before filling each with the Chilean Chardonnay. She handed Carter a glass as they sat side-by-side on the sofa.

"What made you choose a wine from Chile, Carter?"

"Honestly, I didn't think I needed to impress anyone tonight. It was cheap and I really can't tell the difference."

Jeannie raised her glass. "What should we toast to, Inspector?"

Carter thought for a moment. "How about wisdom?"

"May we have it in abundance," she said and clinked her glass with Carter's. "You never told me how you happened to meet Hannah. It's OK if you prefer not to."

"No, I don't mind telling you. We have some time." Carter took a sip of wine. "Where to begin? I had a reputation for finding killers quickly and bringing them in easily. I never had to draw my gun or threaten perps with violence of any sort. It was not that I was all that clever, just lucky, I suppose. There was this guy who murdered his wife and called 9-1-1 to confess. They sent me to arrest him and I guess I was starting to believe my own reputation and got sloppy. The killer's girlfriend was in the house and stabbed me in the back when I cuffed him - just above my right kidney. I was in the hospital for about a month.

Hannah was a nurse there and would clean and dress my wound every day. We would talk about things: her job, Korea and what she liked to do when she wasn't working at the hospital. We continued seeing each other after I was released. We would have coffee in the hospital cafeteria when I came in for checkups. We started dating and the rest is history."

"You mean one part of your history," Jeannie said, having just finished her first glass of Chardonnay. "I don't know much about what came before."

Carter refilled her glass. "Well, how far back do you want to go?"

"I'll leave that up to you. Were you ever married before you met Hannah?"

"Nearly a couple of times, but always to the same woman."

"Now you have me curious. Tell me about it."

"Alright, but it's a bit of an involved story."

Jeannie glanced at her Cartier watch. "We've got time and wine. Go on, I'm listening."

"A long, long time ago I was in law school; Georgetown, in D.C. I was living with my girlfriend who was also a Georgetown law student."

"You were a lawyer?"

"Studying to be, at that point. After we graduated I was recruited by a large New York City law firm and she went to work for a smaller one in Jersey City. I didn't even bother to take the bar exam. I knew corporate law wasn't for me. I quit and figured I had the requirements for the F.B.I. so I applied and was accepted. They shipped me off to the field office here in Minneapolis."

"Whatever happened to your girlfriend?"

"She had passed the Jersey bar and loved her job. She did lots of *pro bono* jobs and even managed to find time for legal aid work. She was a real go-getter, not like me."

Jeannie swallowed the last of the wine in her glass. "Fascinating. So, how did you become Inspector Brand?"

"The F.B.I. was way too bureaucratic and boring for me so I quit and enrolled in the Minneapolis Police Academy.

"You must have been a pretty old rookie, right?"

Carter laughed. "Yeah, I was almost forty years-old. My classmates called me grandpa."

"So, what happened to the girlfriend back in New Jersey?"

"She followed me to Minneapolis but after I left the Bureau she left me; told me I was unable to commit to anything and she had a life to live. Clock was ticking, you know? She did pretty well. Found an old law firm here and became quite an effective litigator. She was so good, in fact, that the governor appointed her as a district judge here in Hennepin County."

Jeannie again clinked Carter's glass with hers and for the next half hour they finished the wine remaining in the bottle, alternately topping off each other's glass.

Carter checked his Timex watch. "Ready to roll some matzo?"

"Ready when you are, CB," Jeannie answered and followed him into the kitchen.

Jeannie took charge of the operation. She turned the flame under the pot of water to high. "The most important thing when rolling matzo balls is to keep your hands moist but not sopping wet. If they're too dry the meal sticks to your hands. Too wet and the ball falls apart."

"Moist hands, check," Carter confirmed after dipping his fingers into the bowl of water Jeannie had set on the counter.

"Gather enough matzo to form a ball about the size of a ping pong ball," Jeannie said, collecting the necessary quantity in her hand. "Now just roll it into a ball - not too hard or you'll squish it - gently, softly, lovingly."

"I didn't know that matzo balls were so delicate," Carter said with a sly grin.

"Well, I think that's been your problem, Inspector. You've been disrespecting your matzo balls. Here, watch, learn." Jeannie pinched a bit of mixture from the bowl, transferred it to her palm and caressed it with slow, circular motions until it formed a perfect sphere, then tossed it into a pot of boiling water.

"Your turn," she said.

Carter shook the excess water off his hands, scooped a dollop of meal and began rolling it between his palms.

Jeannie grasped his top hand firmly between her thumb and fingers and slowly moved it in circles.

"Gently, gently, a little more, almost there...that's it...just like that."

Carter paused before dropping his matzo ball into the pot. "Whew, I never knew making soup could be so, um, satisfying."

"Jesus said that love is all you need in everything you do, including making matzo balls."

"He said that?"

Jeannie giggled. "Maybe not in the Gospels, but I'm sure he would have if asked."

"Well, I must say, they are very handsome matzo balls. We make a great matzo ball rollin' team, Jeannie Park-Reed."

She smiled. "Let these babies simmer for about a half hour and we'll be ready to eat. This is the soup?" Jeannie asked, pointing to a covered pot on a burner adjacent to the simmering matzo balls.

"Yes, but it's a mix, I'm afraid, with some special embellishments: a little extra carrots and some dill weed."

Carter lowered the flame and led Jeannie into the living room. He turned up the music, a soulful Jackie Wilson ballad, and drew her close for a few slow-dance spins before sitting with her on the couch. They shared sections of the newspaper to consume time while the matzo balls simmered. On the back of the *Tribune* second section the headline read "Still No Arrest in Calhoun Slay."

Thirty minutes later, the stove's timer buzzed an alert that the matzo balls were fully cooked. Carter gingerly transferred them one-by-one to the soup pot. "Soup's on!" he announced, but Jeannie was fast asleep on the sofa.

Two hours later, Jeannie stirred, stretched and bolted upright. "Carter, how long have I been asleep?"

"A couple of hours. I let you sleep off the wine before driving home. Let me warm up the soup for you."

"Carter, I've got to run," Jeannie said, hastily gathering her coat and pocketbook. "Read the Bible, every day if you can. Some people who are new to the faith read one chapter from the Old Testament in the morning and one from the New Testament at night." She stood outside the door. "Read the book of Hebrews, Carter. Will you do that for me? Come to my house on Wednesday, OK?" She gave him a quick hug and kiss on the forehead then she was gone.

CHAPTER 14 WIND

CARTER SAT in the Prius running in stealth mode at a curb one block away from number 153 on Fisher Avenue. He could see the tail lights of Jeff Reed's Ford Taurus coming to a stop at the end of the street then turning onto Lincoln. It wasn't necessary for Carter to wait for Jeff to leave for his Wednesday youth group meeting, but he just felt more comfortable alone with Jeannie. Jeff was a quirky guy who could be funny on occasion - at least he was funny to Carter, whether his funniness was intentional or not - yet, just as often, gave Carter the creeps at his indifference to Jeannie's obvious affection towards him.

He rolled the Prius silently down Fisher Avenue and pulled into Jeannie's driveway. She was waiting for him on the front stoop in baggy sweat pants and plain, white sweatshirt, a bottle of spring water in her hand. She smiled her radiant smile, like a lighthouse beacon guiding him to the door.

"Sorry I'm so late, Jeannie," Carter said. "I had some personal business to attend to. It's pretty chilly tonight, aren't you cold dressed like that?"

"Nope, I just got back from a jog. I'm sweating like a

pig. Come on in. I made some *hamul pajun* for us to snack on." She opened the door and led him inside.

Carter took a seat at the table while Jeannie disappeared into the kitchen, returning a few minutes later holding a silvery teapot by its handle and a plate of the Korean seafood pancake cut into eight pizza-shaped slices. On the table in front of Carter sat a medium-size porcelain bowl with two smaller ones and two teaspoons next to it. She filled the larger bowl halfway with a milky-white liquid from the teapot and ladled portions into the small bowls.

"Give it a stir first," she said and lifted one of the bowls to eye level. "*Gun Bae*" she toasted, and clinked her bowl against Carter's.

"What are we drinking tonight?"

"*Makguli*, rice wine."

"Like *soju*?"

"No, *soju* is for drunks. *Makguli* has flavor, more refined." She took a sip then groped for the right words. "Carter, would it be too personal if I asked if the personal business that delayed you tonight involved Hannah?"

"No, it's alright. I don't mind talking about it with you. In fact, I would be grateful." Carter returned the *makguli* bowl to his lips and did not put it down until he had drained its remaining contents. "I got a call from my sister earlier today informing me that our father had passed away."

Jeannie took Carter's hand. "Oh, I'm so sorry. Was it sudden?"

"Couldn't tell you, Jeannie. I hadn't spoken to him in years. We were never very close when I was growing up. He is...was...a professional piano player. He was good, but there are lots of good pianists in the world and there was really nothing special about his talent. He possessed an oversized ego and took work that he felt was beneath him only when the family was broke, which was most of the time. He was the stereotypical American self-hating Jew who denied his heritage but felt a sense of pride when celebrities were found to be Jewish or when the conversation included Hitler or The Holocaust. Very strange.

My mom raised my sister and me by herself after he left. He never bothered to find out how we were and I never had any desire to hear from him. I was not moved in the least hearing that he had died. For me, he had died long ago." Even though Carter's head was bowed as he recalled childhood memories of his father, Jeannie noticed a tear form and run down his cheek. She rubbed his back warmly. He lifted his head.

"Jeannie, lately, after all my years as a cop, I've been thinking how futile it's all been. The wealthy and poor, the upstanding and evil, all end up exactly the same. No matter who we are or what we accomplish in life our destiny is always the same. It's like we're all deluding ourselves that anything we do has any meaning whatsoever. I mean, aren't we just performing on God's stage for his amusement? Ultimately, does anything we do really matter? Is even the most horrible crime or the greatest act of charity any more significant than a passing gust of wind off the lake?"

"Whew! That's a pretty heavy human burden to carry around. So don't. Unload it to Jesus and remember what he taught us so clearly in the Gospels: Thy kingdom come on Earth as it is in heaven. On Earth, Carter. That is where we are right now and all we can do is enjoy every minute we have left. There is a time and place for everything. Right now the time is for us to be together pondering God's word and eating good food and drinking good Korean wine. Right now, for you and me nothing else matters. Do you fear God and try to keep his commandments?"

"I do, Jeannie. I haven't been leading an exemplary life lately, and from this point in my life forward, I want to, more than anything."

But had he really been trying to keep God's commandments? He reflected on chapter 22 of the book of Matthew where Jesus declares the top commandments are "loving God with all your heart" and "loving your neighbor as yourself", in that order. If the Son of God recognized nuances in the term, "love" he did not communicate it in the Gospels and Carter was not inclined to get legalistic with the words of Jesus. Even if he could legitimize his affection for Jeannie through that passage it was certainly invalidated by his present lack of love for himself.

She took his hand in hers. "Enjoy the *makguli* and *pajun*. It will keep your thoughts away from stressing over the unknown. There is only now."

"You're right. You're always right and when I'm with you I feel so right and don't think about anything else but being with you."

Jeannie smiled and ladled another portion of *makguli* into Carter's bowl. She dipped a wedge of *pajun* in soy sauce, nibbled it, and placed it back onto the dish. "Carter, everyone at Gethsemane is so shocked at Dr. Kang's murder. I've been told that some people are so frightened that they won't even come to church until the killer is caught."

"Why is that?" Carter asked between sips of wine.

"It's no secret that Dr. Kang was committed to disgracing Pastor Choi in order to shame him into resigning.

He had his supporters and some enemies, too. Some people are afraid that since they were known to side with Dr. Kang that harm might come to them as well."

"You can't be serious. They really think that Kang was killed by someone from Gethsemane?"

"I know, it sounds ludicrous, but Korean's can be very passionate people and sometimes they lose touch with their rationality."

"I'll keep that in mind, Jeannie, but Kang had more than a few enemies outside the church. I find it unlikely that a congregation of God-fearing, Christ-following people would resort to murder to resolve a church management issue."

Carter picked up the last slice if *pajun*. "Would it be rude if I finished the *pajun*? It was really good. I can't recall Hannah ever making it so well."

"Sure, go right ahead. I think the Korean soy sauce makes the difference." Jeannie waited for Carter to swallow the last bite. "I'm sorry. I'm being such a nosy ninny tonight. Is there anything you can tell me about the case that might put people's minds at ease?"

"Not really. We're looking at the people Kang had a professional relationship with - patients, associates; the people close to him that he had problems with in the past." With a cloth napkin, Carter wiped his fingers clean. "That was very tasty," Carter said rubbing his hands together. "What chapter are we reading tonight?"

Jeannie put her hands to her forehead. "Forgive me, Carter. I was planning for us to read Revelations but I'm starting to feel a bit light-headed. Can we continue this tomorrow? Will you pick me up behind the church tomorrow night? Eight o'clock?"

CHAPTER 15 CRUISE

THE BLINKING TRAFFIC light turned the rain-soaked windshield into an aquarelle as Carter gently braked the Prius to a halt one block from Gethsemane church. The wipers were set to the slowest interval and each squealing cycle was like a Greek chorus imploring him not to go.

Carter signaled a left turn into the church parking lot and switched the wipers to a constant sweep to keep up with the rain's growing intensity. He strained to find Jeannie under the sanctuary's backdoor awning hoping that she would be there and silently praying that she would not.

But there she was, pulling tight her trench coat lapels to keep out the night chill. Carter pulled up next to her and reached across the front seat to push open the passenger door. In one motion, she escaped the awning's shelter and dipped into the warm automobile. The moist air dampened her usually well-groomed hair and was now collected in a loose pony-tail bound by a turquoise tie. She wore no makeup but in the half-darkness her profile became a lovely cameo. With a weak smile, she buckled her shoulder belt and sank into the seat, her sight fixed towards the floor. Carter returned the smile equally.

Neither of them knew where they were going nor would they risk a suggestion. Carter made a right turn onto 27 North and cruised along at barely the speed limit. Jeannie looked ahead hoping to get a hint of their destination as they continued down the highway.

Passing a trucker's motel, he stole a peek at Jeannie. She made no indication. They cruised on. Several towns down the highway they approached a Hyatt Hotel. Carter signaled to turn into the entrance.

"Hungry?" he asked. Jeannie shook her head no. "Should we get a drink?" Jeannie declined, expressionless.

Carter had no idea what they were doing that evening or why Jeannie wanted to see him. It was maddening. To escape the silent anticipation he turned his thoughts to his chosen profession.

Why did civilized people kill other people? How could a devout Christian kill another human being? How could sane people who otherwise deplore violence and murder find it entertaining at the same time? As a species, having essentially conquered its natural predators, are we drawn to conflict and war to keep our human population in check? Is there something in our evolved DNA that compels us to kill for the preservation of the race? If such insanity as murder could be rationalized as sane, natural and inevitable, could being mindlessly drawn to Jeannie not be similarly understood?

Carter pulled back onto 27 and headed south. Ten silent miles later he cautiously took the exit for Riverside well aware of the local police policy of ticketing cars for even the slightest speed limit infraction.

The house was dark as they pulled up to the curb outside 153 Fisher Avenue. Carter turned off the engine.

71

They both sat silently. After a few moments, Carter reached over, took her hand and pulled her close to him. He held her tightly and sat silently with the fear that if he let go they would never hold each other again. Carter kissed her forehead. She smiled the same half-sad smile as when they met earlier in the evening. She opened the door and walked quickly to the front steps leaving the car door open behind her.

CHAPTER 16 IPSEITY

THE CASE WAS unfolding easily and Carter knew that in such circumstances he should have been sharpening his efforts, like a pilot focusing attention on his aircraft while descending from cruising altitude to final approach. He was not.

Instead of considering the veracity of Benezek's alibi he could think only of how looking into Jeannie's chestnut-brown eyes made him melt. Just as John Lennon never realized what a kiss could be, Carter came to know the power of Jeannie Park-Reed's soul-melding embrace. Rather than pondering the plausibility of Jason's Tiffani theory his mind was prisoner to the memory of Jeannie's soft voice and incapacitating smile. It seemed like every waking minute was dominated by the anticipation of being close to her.

He craved her affection. For him, she was not just filling the emotional vacuum of Hannah's departure but providing the spiritual engagement he never found in marriage. He was falling in love with Jeannie Park-Reed and the more he tried to convince himself that he was not the more he recognized the futility of resistance. He was a man of good character and integrity who, nonetheless, had become addicted to JPR like he was addicted to air.

The situation was absurd in every respect: he was still a married, faithful, Christian man and she was the bride of a pastor – a *samonim*. His normally disciplined emotions were no longer contained in the hardened silo of his professional ethos. He was flaming, hurtling, space junk helpless to fight the inexorable pull of Jeannie Park-Reed's gravity.

Before she came into his life he possessed a workable sense of self framed by his introduction to the Gospels through his marriage to Hannah. She, the scriptures and his work formed the tether that kept his irresolute nature from spinning his life out of control. Now, one of the cords was gone leaving just his faith and his occupation as the axes of his existence.

The vibrating Blackberry danced across Carter's desk.

FROM: JKIM

TO: INSP. BRAND

SUBJ: KANG CASE

KANG SUV FOUND N 25 AVE. DRIVER ARRESTED -KIM

CHAPTER 17 CALVIN

THE MEAGER FOLDER of documents that was Calvin
Chennault to the Minneapolis penal system told Carter that
the suspect sitting handcuffed in front of him was not likely
the killer of Dr. Kang. A nineteen year old light-skinned
African-American, he was of medium height, thin, but not
skinny, with a physical countenance indicating an upbringing
that was not deprived of middle class advantages. He was
well dressed in a casual style more likely to be seen in a golf
course clubhouse than in the working class black
neighborhood in which he was apprehended.

Carter straddled a steel folding chair backwards resting
his arms on the frame top. Calvin sat slumped on a chair
next to his.

Carter began calmly. "You're a good kid, Calvin, so
how is it that we found you behind the wheel of a stolen
SUV with another man's wallet in your possession?"

Chennault matched Carter's relaxed tone. "Why should
it surprise you?"

"Well, because it says here that you were only charged
with a crime once and that was for stealing a Cross Century

75

pen from Weinberger's. Quite a leap from ripping off expensive pens to grand theft auto, don't you think?"

Chennault managed a confident smile. "Until we're caught, aren't we all basically self-serving?"

Carter was neither willing nor prepared to engage a young perp in a discussion of moral philosophy but decided to play a few rounds to get the conversation on track. "That's right, Calvin, but since you were caught, wouldn't you agree that it would be more self serving for you to cooperate?"

"What do you want to know?"

Instincts told Carter to step carefully through the interrogation. Chennault was bright - maybe brighter than he - and he knew that his young suspect would remain forthcoming as long as Carter respectfully regarded him as an intellectual equal. "Would you like to explain how the vehicle and wallet came into your possession?"

"Obviously, I stole them."

"Yes, that is quite obvious, Calvin, would you care to elaborate?"

Chennault paused to consider his response - like a pool shark choosing the best shot on a congested table that might leave him setup for the next one.

"I found them."

Carter remained nonreactive. "Found them where, Calvin?"

The young man appeared to be growing tired of the inane banter. He exhaled. "A white man stepped out of the SUV on North Ninth. He left the engine running and the doors unlocked. He walked right passed me. He looked at me and then at the SUV like he was inviting me to steal it.

He walked down the street and lit up a cigarette at the corner. I waited awhile, maybe five minutes, to see if he was coming back. He just stood there smoking the cigarette. I walked over to the SUV and got in on the passenger side. I moved over to the driver's seat and watched the guy through the rearview mirror. I saw the wallet on the console. It had cash and credit cards. The guy lit up another cigarette, like he was waiting for someone, so I put the car in gear and drove away."

Chennault had made no effort to flee when the patrol car signaled for him to pull over. He had not resisted at all when arrested. Here was a peculiar individual who, apparently, placed high value on his integrity yet could rationally, unapologetically steal a car; either that or he was the most cunning thief Carter had ever encountered. But without a significant criminal record Carter was inclined to believe the story.

"What did the guy look like?"

"He was kind of tall, about your height, maybe a little bit taller. He had a beard and mustache. Wore an army coat, with a hood. And he wore glasses."

Carter immediately thought about his guest in the Hennepin County lockup, Donald Benezek. It made sense: kill Kang and setup a black guy. Maybe it made too much sense, too easy. But Benezek and Jessica were hardly criminal geniuses so it wasn't such an unlikely scenario.

It was early evening by the time Jason arranged a lineup for Chennault to view. Benezek stood stone-faced on the far right side of a three-man row. Chennault watched from behind a one-way mirror.

"Do any of them look familiar, Calvin?"

"Hard to tell. He was pretty far away."

Through the intercom, Jason ordered the group to turn to their right. Benezek's eyelids twitched nervously.

"I think it could be the guy on the right," Chennault said tentatively.

"Not sure?"

"Pretty sure."

CHAPTER 18 UNI

THE LAST THING Carter wanted to do that night was to re-interview Benezek. Even with Chennault's uncertainty, he felt he could get a quick confession the next day, send the case to the DA and have a legitimate reason to be with Jeannie that night. He imagined how she would smile as he proudly reported how he - her hero - solved the case and captured the dangerous villain. He would be her knight in shining armor humbly presenting himself for his reward.

Nervous as a high school sophomore asking for his first date, he phoned Jeannie. After five rings the answering machine picked up:

This is Jeff, please leave a message and we'll call you back
<beep>

Carter's scripted and memorized speech was now useless. He fumbled for words cognizant of the risk that they might be heard by Jeffery Reed.

"Hi Jeannie, this is Carter. Have some great news..."

Jeannie answered, breathlessly. "Carter? Hi, I'm home, what's going on?"

Carter blossomed. "We had a big breakthrough in the case today. Will you be home later? Can I stop by?"

She answered after a pause, "Sure, I guess. What time?"

"Is eight-thirty too late? Can we get some dinner?"

Jeannie accepted willingly, but cautiously. "OK. "What kind of food are you hungry for?"

"I'm thinking Japanese tonight. There's a new place that just opened on West Lake, *Takamatsu*. Have you heard anything about it?"

"Yep, run by Koreans. It's fine if you like your sashimi dry and your meat overcooked. How about *Koshi* on North Seventh?"

"You're on. What time should I pick you up? Jeff will join us, of course?" Carter stipulated to remove any suggestion of improper intention.

"He has youth Bible study this evening but it's fine, he won't mind. He's not that fond of Japanese food, anyway."

"Eight-thirty it is. I'll call for a reservation."

Carter placed the phone's receiver back in its cradle. He had just stepped on a fast-moving walkway in a dark tunnel that led straight to Jeannie Park-Reed. Was he out of his mind? Of course he was - his rational mind had nothing to do with this obsession. He jotted down all the man-woman attraction states he could think of: flirtation, affection, infatuation, passion, friendship, sex, love, romance. Did his current state of mind fit into any of those categories? If he considered himself safe today would he still be when the pitiful suitcase of his life dropped into the JPR luggage carousel? It did not matter. He was insane and knew that holding tight to his thin Christian faith would be his only salvation.

Carter arrived at 153 Fisher Avenue fifteen minutes early. He bounded the stoop and rang the doorbell in one motion.

"Come on in," Jeannie called out. "I'll be out in a sec."

"Take your time," Carter called back. "I'm early."

Carter had never been beyond the dining room in his three previous visits. The hallway wall leading to the bedrooms was sparsely covered with a pastiche of photographs and scripture verses imprecisely mounted in K-Mart-grade do-it-yourself plastic frames. Starting a few feet past the bathroom door, he did quick studies of each picture before moving to the next group down the hall.

There was the standard wedding shot of Jeannie and Jeff stuffing cake in each other's mouths, he in a tux and she in a strapless satin gown; verses eight through twelve of the 103rd Psalm printed on faux parchment; Psalm 149:6 printed in plain serif-less type mounted in a frame much longer than it was wide reaching from eye level to almost the floor:

May the praise of God be in their mouths and a double-edged sword in their hands.

The wall hangings continued past an open bedroom door. Instinctively glancing inside, he found a desk and computer monitor with random fractal patterns tracing the screen. Directly across from that were a three-drawer dresser and one double bed - just one. On top of the dresser Carter spotted a pair of black, wire rimmed glasses which seemed strange to him since he had never noticed Jeff nor Jeannie wearing glasses. He stepped out.

Across the hallway, he cracked open the door. Peeking inside, he did a quick survey of the contents: vanity, dresser and one double bed. He closed the door and stepped back across the hall into the first bedroom. He tried on the glasses. There was no apparent magnification. As his over-fifty eyes were not even close to 20-20 he dismissed any spot conclusions. He turned to leave the room. Jeannie was standing in the doorway staring straight at him, not smiling. He froze corpse cold.

Carter could hear a car approach on Fisher Avenue and followed its sound until it faded away in the distance, then another vehicle Dopplered past. "I'm sorry. I didn't mean to intrude. I was..."

Jeannie cut him short. "That is Jeffrey's bed. My room is across the hall. Carter, we don't sleep together. May we go? I'm starved."

That was more information than Carter could absorb at that moment. He was so on his heels that he had not noticed how stupefyingly beautiful Jeannie was that evening dressed in a form-fitting, black embroidered dress with a mandarin collar; her hair styled up in a bun secured with cloisonné *hashi* sticks. Carter moved to lead her to the front door. She kissed his cheek and quickly wiped off the lipstick like a mother cleaning her child's face with spit after dropping him off at Kindergarten. At the front door, Carter stepped into scuffed Rockport loafers while Jeannie slipped into exquisite Dolce and Gabbana pumps.

Things were clearly out of Carter's control. Their get-together that night was not going to be an innocent, friendly celebration with a woman whose company he had come to enjoy. This was a date, something for which he longed but was totally unprepared for. He wasn't a vain man, never feeling intimidated by those with far greater physical or financial assets. He was a reasonably handsome, fairly-religious man with reasonably good income from a respectable job that formed the basis of his respectable middle-aged identity. But right then, he was a casually-attired married man about to drive off with a dressed-to-kill married woman in a funny-looking, environmentally-friendly vehicle encrusted with road salt.

The escalator of his life had been switched to fast but he had no idea in which direction it was going.

Twenty-five minutes later, they arrived at the restaurant. Finding no empty spaces in the restaurant's parking lot, Carter reluctantly queued in the valet parking line fully aware of how ridiculously mismatched he and Jeannie would appear. He shifted into park, moved quickly around to the passenger door, which Jeannie had already opened, and presented his hand to escort her into the restaurant. She swiveled towards him and lifted herself up and out in one fluid motion, smoothing her dress as she took his arm.

They were seated immediately in the small *tatami* room Carter had reserved, available only because it was an atypically light Friday evening. Since leaving her house Carter sensed there was something troubling on Jeannie's mind. Her usually incandescent smile was now Mona Lisa.

Right away, a kimono-clad waitress came by for their drink order. Jeannie gave hers in Japanese. "*Ba-bon*, Jim Beam, *o onegaishimasu,*"

"*Biru*, Kirin," Carter matched weakly. "Jeannie, I might be celebrating prematurely but we're pretty sure the Kang case is in the bag," Carter said, hoping his ebullience would brighten Jeannie's mood.

"I'm sorry, Carter, you're such a nice guy and I so much enjoy the times we've been having together but...this is so unfair of me." Jeannie faltered, restraining tears.

He reached over the table and cupped her hands "What's wrong, Jeannie?"

"Carter, I consider myself a righteous Christian woman and a proper pastor's wife. But...I am so lonely," she said, dabbing a tear with her cloth napkin. "Jeffrey and I have not been close in a very long time. He is very passionate about his faith but, well, not very about me...women...do you understand?"

He held her hands warmly, sympathetically. He didn't really understand what she was saying and was not sure why she was saying it to him. She was in need of emotional succor but feeling pitiful himself he had none to offer. Jeannie had opened a gate leaving only Carter's tortured integrity between them.

The waitress returned with their drinks and poured the beer smoothly down the side of Carter's oversized, Kirin-branded glass, skillfully controlling the height and width of the rising foam.

"A pro," Jeannie sniffled, and raised her glass to clink a toast. Regaining her composure, Jeannie took a sip of her potent liquor and brightened. "I'm sorry, Carter, we came here to celebrate your inspectorial brilliance and here I am getting all mawkish on you. I am famished. Let's order." Jeannie gestured to the waitress. *Sumimasen, chuumon onegai shimasu?"*

When the waitress arrived, Carter ordered the deluxe sushi entree and Jeannie went for the off-menu *torafugu*.

"So, tell me, Inspector, how did you catch the villain?"

Carter absolutely knew he should not discuss with anyone a case in progress, especially with an individual so close to it as Jeannie Park-Reed was, but felt unable to hold anything back after she had been so emotionally unreserved. He took a gulp of beer.

"We located Kang's SUV. We believe his nurse and her boyfriend were selling drugs bought with prescriptions that he provided. We're not sure of the details yet but the evidence indicates they killed him. Maybe he refused to supply them, maybe he demanded sex in return, don't know yet...soon."

As soon as the words left his lips, Carter knew he had screwed up. Beautiful, sad, vulnerable Jeannie had disabled all of his professional circuit breakers and he could only beg for her discretion. "Jeannie, this is all very confidential, of course, so please keep this just between us." Jeannie took a final sip of her bourbon and pantomimed zippering her lips as their dinners were served.

With Japanese *hashi* sticks, Carter deftly handled a *hamachi negiri* oversoaked in wasabi-infused soy sauce. As he put it to his lips he noticed Jeannie muttering to herself a prayer of grace in Korean, eyes closed, head bowed. He placed the sushi back in the plate and bowed his head as well.

"I'm sorry, Jeannie," he said after her "amen." "I'm not used to saying grace without being led, especially at a restaurant."

"That's alright; it was rude of me not to include you. It looks like they gave you quite an assortment."

"Yes, I ordered the deluxe. It comes with *uni* which I really don't care for."

"Why? It's considered a delicacy, you know."

"I know, but it's pretty smellish, like something you might find stuck to the bottom of your swimming pool."

Jeannie laughed. "Smellish? Is that like stinkish?"

Carter realized that he had unconsciously used the adjective he once heard Hannah use instead of 'smelly' and liked it so much better that it had become part of their private lexicon.

Without being requested, their check was delivered; not by the traditionally-dressed waitress, but by a suited older man who Carter assumed was the manager politely hinting that the place was closing and that they should think about leaving soon. This was confirmed by the sight of idle waitresses, busboys and sushi chefs anxiously waiting to claim their stake in the night's last gratuity.

The visibly annoyed parking attendant was checking his watch as Carter requested the Prius. He could see the words "Wash me please!" scrawled on the salted rear door panel as his car rolled up. He looked at the graffiti, then at the young man who had fetched his ride, then handed him an extra buck to acknowledge his own share of responsibility for the petty vandalism.

As they exited the parking lot, Carter asked "Would you mind if we listened to some music on the way home?" When Jeannie did not respond, he glanced over to see her already asleep curled up in as much space as the shoulder harness would allow. Blindly sifting through the hamburger wrappers, unopened junk mail and ATM receipts in the car's console space, he located the CD that had become as permanent a fixture in the car as the CD player itself: a Frank Sinatra retrospective from his years with the Capitol records label. Carter slid the disk into the slot and switched it to shuffle mode. Sinatra's smooth baritone rose above the strings: "...you lie awake and think about the girl but never, ever think of counting sheep." Frank was singing to him as he was singing along to Jeannie.

"*Umma, anyo, anyo*," Jeannie mumbled softly while asleep in her seat. "*UMMA, ANYO! ADJASHEE ANYO!*" she cried still asleep, her voice filled with desperation. Carter pulled over to the curb. "*Neh, Umma, neh,*" she sobbed plaintively and then she was asleep again.

Even with Carter's limited Korean vocabulary, he understood the simple words that escaped from Jeannie's dream: "Mother, no, no. Mister, no, no. Yes, mother, yes." Carter switched the CD mode to repeat and let the album play again and again while Jeannie slept. He turned off the engine, loosened his tie and closed his eyes as well.

He was awakened by a flock of chirping birds welcoming the dawn using the Prius as a target for their morning droppings. Although the car was still almost six blocks from 153 Fisher Avenue Jeannie was already gone.

CHAPTER 19 A VERY LONG DAY

IT WAS AFTER six AM when Carter surfaced from his condo's underground parking garage, a wrinkled rain coat double-folded in his arms. Grungy and stiff from spending a frigid night in the Prius, his muscles felt all of his fifty-one years. He fumbled for the building key, first in his jacket pockets, then in his pants and finally in the pockets of the trench coat.

"Hey you!" the owner of a gravelly voice barked at him from behind and shoved him so hard he stumbled forward barely able to stay on his feet. He whirled around just as a fist was about to hit its mark on his left kidney, smashing him instead squarely in the solar plexus. He doubled over in pain, gasping for wind.

"C'mon, you bastard, you got more comin'!" said the rage-filled voice. It was Perry Johnson wearing an unzipped parka, a guinea-T and low-hanging Everlast boxing shorts, fists maneuvering for the next punch.

"Johnson, what the hell are you doing?" Carter groaned, his hands held out defensively.

"C'mon you slimy dog, take your medicine like a man. Who's the clever skunk now? Little different when you go up against a man, ain't it, you laughin' leech!"

For a brief moment he thought about how Jeannie would snicker at Perry Johnson's torrent of mixed metaphors but realized that Mr. Johnson was quite serious about demonstrating that an octogenarian former boxer could still deliver a serious ass whooping and that he should respond accordingly.

Johnson unleashed a straight right. Carter took the shot on his outstretched hands. While age might have slowed the man's delivery the blow struck flesh and bone hard like the electric pain of a major league baseball striking a bat.

"Shit!" Carter yelled, shaking the sting out of his hands. "What's with you?"

As much as Carter preferred to avoid violence, especially directed at a man old enough to be his father, this old man was on a mission to put a major hurt on him so he prepared for a short tussle. So he hoped.

Johnson lunged at Carter's midsection knocking him to the pavement, hard, on his left hip. Carter rose painfully to his feet. They jabbed. They wrestled. Carter threw Johnson to the ground and did a quick frisk of his clothing for handcuffs. Not found, he limped to his trench coat on the sidewalk and located his steel braces in an inside pocket. Johnson creaked semi-vertical and dove weakly at Carter who redirected him back to the ground and slapped on the cuffs.

Johnson remained prone and panting on the sidewalk. Carter, also breathing heavily, sat down next to him.

Perry Johnson wept. "You didn't beat me, Brand. You couldn't beat me without those bracelets."

"I should run you in, Perry, but I suspect that's what you want, isn't it?" Carter asked, rubbing his bruised hip.

"You're a real smart dick, Brand. How did you figure out so quick I killed that doctor? Where did I screw up?"

Carter stopped massaging his hip. "Perry, you didn't kill Dr. Kang."

"I did too! I beat that lousy Chinaman with my fists 'til he begged me for mercy then I punched him some more 'til he stopped wailing like a baby!"

"He was shot, Perry."

Johnson paused. "Yeah, that's right. I beat him bloody then shot him with a gun!"

"There were no signs of a struggle," Carter said, even more sympathetically.

Johnson lifted his head just high enough to watch an ancient black Cadillac Coupe de Ville screech away from its parking space across the street. "I assume that was your wheelman, Tiffani, driving off?" Carter asked gently. Johnson nodded slowly, his head resting profile on the concrete pavement. "Perry, I'm going to take off the cuffs but you have to promise you'll behave and go home. Is that a deal?"

"What for? I'm nothing, Brand. I can't even get myself arrested."

CHAPTER 20 NOT SO FAST

THE FIRST FEW bars of the old Peter Gunn TV show's theme song sounded the voicemail ringtone on Carter's Blackberry. He pressed the green call button to retrieve the message. It was frantic:

"Boss, Jason here. Call my cell."

Carter's heart raced. His obsession with Jeannie Park-Reed was jeopardizing the one thing in his life that was predictable, strong and resilient: his profession. He dialed Jason.

"Sgt. Kim," Jason answered, using his all-business salutation.

"Jason, it's Brand. What's going on?"

"Where have you been? I've been calling and texting for hours." Carter checked the Blackberry's received messages queue and verified six unanswered messages of various types since 1:00 AM. "Never mind, their alibi checks out. At the time of Kang's murder their car was being ticketed on I-5 for a busted brake light ten miles from Lake Calhoun. We're still holding them on the drug charges."

"I'll be there in twenty minutes," Carter said and staggered out the door and down the stairs to his car.

On the way to the station, Carter stopped at a pharmacy to buy a cane; just a simple hook-handled wooden cane to help keep the weight off his bruised left hip. He rolled the Prius into the station parking deck driving up the ramp to his reserved space on the third floor. Remembering that his boss was on vacation, he circled back to the first floor and pulled into his manager's space. For the next few days he would be Captain Izzy Cohen to the parking garage staff.

Jason was waiting for him when Carter hobbled into his office. "What happened to you?" Jason asked, upon seeing his enfeebled partner.

"Well, you were half right about the Johnsons," Carter replied, easing himself gingerly into his swivel chair.

"Care to explain?"

"I'll tell you later. Where do we stand with the lovebirds?"

"They're in with ADA Campion and their lawyers. She's looking to get a solid case against them for illegally obtaining and selling narcotics. Since Kang was the undisputed provider of the 'scripts, and he's dead, she's not too interested right now in expanding the investigation. She wants a quick, effortless conviction for the drugs."

"OK, so where does that leave us?"

"Last night I took the liberty of re-interviewing them both after you left. Jessica said she had gotten a call from a female looking to buy a grand worth of Oxy. She said the woman spoke to her in Korean and called herself 'Suzy'. They agreed to meet uptown. The woman told them to look for a white Lexus SUV on the corner of Colfax and 33.

On the way they got pulled over by highway patrol and given a summons for a broken brake light so they got there late and didn't see the SUV at the agreed upon corner. They cruised around awhile and spotted it at a light on Lake. They weren't sure if it was the right SUV since the driver was a man and not a woman but Benezek gestured to the driver to pull over. They got in the SUV and completed the transaction, which would explain the large amount of cash we found in their house, though that would not be unusual if they were dealing pills regularly. We pulled Ahn's and Benezek's prints off the SUV's door handle and console. The strange thing is that the only other good prints we found were matched to Chennault and Kang."

"It makes sense that Kang's SUV would be in that neighborhood. Look how close it is to where he was killed. They lured him to Lake Calhoun, killed him, probably relieving him of any cash in his wallet, bought drugs with the money and tried to setup someone locally for the murder. That someone was Calvin. We have to find that Suzy and her partner.

Jason smiled, "And that's why you're a legend, boss, where do we go from here?"

"The SUV," Carter instructed without hesitation.

CHAPTER 21 SEEKING SUZY

JASON STUDIED the list of evidence found to date, each item appearing under a heading indicating where it was found. He read the document to Carter.

"In the SUV we lifted prints of Benezek, Ahn, Calvin and Kang. Other than theirs, there were none that we could easily identify. From Calvin we recovered Kang's wallet, keys and cell phone. From Jessica we found..."

Carter stopped him. "Whose cell phone?"

"It's registered to Kang through AT&T. It's a camera phone but we didn't find any pictures or video recorded."

"How about the calls sent or received?"

"There were a few numbers logged in the phone and some unlisted were received. We're getting the call history and reverse lookups from AT&T."

"Good. We need to find out how this 'Suzy' knew to call Benezek for drugs. Did you have them look at mug shots?"

"Yes, but none were picked out. Benezek was probably known on the street as a source for pharmaceuticals so it wouldn't surprise me if the buyers were total strangers, possibly college students."

"That's true, but he had to have been known to the person who had a motive to kill Kang. Not likely college kids cramming for finals." Carter had been so absorbed with Jeannie Park-Reed recently that he had completely taken his eye off the ball allowing him and Jason to fall into rookie traps. It was time to clear any sentimental thoughts of Jeannie from his mind and start from the beginning. There was a cold-blooded killer on the loose and it was Carter's job to catch him.

He had taken himself and Jason down blind alleys by pursuing logical leads produced through a standard professional approach instead of listening to his gut.

"Let's step back. We've been investigating the Kang we didn't know. What do we really know about him?"

"We know he was single and, if Miss Ahn can be believed, Kang was a pretty sleazy guy," Jason said.

"If she is telling the truth he was more than just a slime ball. If Kang had not settled the harassment suit and she had turned him in for the drugs, he would be doing long jail time now."

"Right, but he would still be alive and they all would probably be in prison."

"It was a stable situation. Kang had more incentive to silence those two than they had to kill him. He was their golden goose."

"Maybe his sex-for-drugs racket didn't start with Jessica," Jason suggested.

"Maybe, but we're still focused on that racket as the motive for his murder, even if the cast of characters was different. What other game might Kang have been playing that ended up with him dead?"

"You're thinking that he pushed his luck too far with a better game player?"

"That's just what I'm thinking."

"So, where to now, boss?"

"First the SUV. Then we widen the scope of our research on Kang beyond the obvious. Something is staring us in the face and we're not seeing it."

The day before Kang's death Carter had observed his public church tirade but never followed up on it, dismissing out of hand any notion that a member or members of Gethsemane could be involved, directly or indirectly, in Kang's murder. Uncomfortable as he knew it would be, it was time to interview those who might have the best knowledge of the Gethsemane church controversy.

CHAPTER 22 WORTH REPEATING

JEANNIE WAS ALREADY sitting at a table in a far corner of the doughnut shop when Carter walked in.

"I ordered coffee for you, Carter. Cream, no sugar, right? It should still be hot. And I bought a few doughnuts; Old fashioned plain OK?"

"Old fashioned and plain? Is that how you see me?" Carter asked with a smile.

"Old fashioned, but fortunately not plain. What can I do for you today, Inspector? Ask away."

Carter lifted the lid off his coffee cup and stirred it slowly. "Do you remember a few weeks back, after Dr. Kang made that scene in the sanctuary, I asked you what he was screaming about? Do you remember? You assured me that it was nothing of any consequence. I let it go as just something that a non-Korean would not understand or wouldn't be interested in. Remember?"

Jeannie crossed her legs and shifted in her seat thirty degrees. She paused to consider her response. "I understand why you would want to know but, honestly, I really don't recall. I remember the outburst but tuned it out and ended the translation. I hope you're not mad at me."

Carter wasn't angry, but he was slipping uncomfortably into a place he was hoping he would not have to go. Jeannie knew perfectly well what Kang was shouting about and he was certain she had a reason not to reveal it. He would have to get that information from some other person or persons at Gethsemane which would not be very easy considering how suspiciously the Korean membership regarded those outside the Korean community. And every interaction he would have with Jeannie from then on would be analyzed for motive – hers by him and his by her.

Carter wet the edge of a donut with the coffee in his cup. "Not a problem, I ask mostly out of curiosity."

CHAPTER 23 SIFTING JANE

"YOU WANT *WASHEE?*" Jane Lee asked in her Hair Palace Unisex Beauty Salon, her scissors and clippers at the ready. "How about foot *massagee?* My girl *duza* good job."

"No thanks, Jane, just a trim today," Carter answered politely. Jane's English was good, but she steadfastly clung to her heavy Korean accent to keep in harmony with her largely Korean clientele.

"I haven't seen you here in long time, *Bwand.* You find *cheapa* place?"

"Cheaper than you, Jane? Impossible."

"You funny guy, *Bwand.* How come you not comedian? You *pwitty bwave* to insult Korean woman with pair of *shop scissah* at you neck," Jane said with a naughty smile and gave Carter a quick scissor prick to the back of his neck to show she meant business.

"Ouch! OK, I deserved that. We're even now?"

Jane clipped silently for a few minutes then asked as if she had been waiting for the right moment "*Yawr pwitty* wife left you, *wight?* I haven't seen her in *churchee* in weeks," she said, while continuing to clip. "It's OK, I *undastan.* Next year I going to *ree-ti-ah*, sell *Haya Parace*, leave lazy husband finally.

So why she left you, *Bwand?* You a good *wooking* man, got good job." Jane lowered her voice to a whisper. "You *make-ah* love good? They *hav-a* pill if you *hav-a pwoblem.*"

"No, Jane, we had no problem there but thanks for the advice." Finding his own opportune moment Carter asked, "Speaking of problems, you've been going to Gethsemane as long as anyone. What do you know about the late Dr. Kang?"

"Oh, he was good Christian man. *Gave-ah* tithe to *churchee. Moksanim* liked him."

"Do you know what he was shouting about in church a week before he was killed?"

"I go to early service so I didn't hear. *Evwyone* knows he had hot *tempa,* though. Someone told me he say *Moksanim* was wasting *constwuction* money but he didn't have *pwoof.*"

"What do you think?"

"You know, I shouldn't say, I don't like to *staht lumor,* but *peeple* say *Moksanim wuz* taking money *fwum da* building *contwactors — kick-a-downs.*"

"You mean kickbacks?"

"*Whatevah.*"

"What do you personally think, Jane?"

Jane switched off the clippers. "I *heah* things but *just-a* lady *talkee,* I think. That Jeannie Pak *vewy* close to *Moksanim;* She *knowz-a ev-ely-thing.* She talk to *biwlders* cause *hehr Engrish* so good, his *not-a* as good."

Jane switched off the clippers, picked up scissors and snipped a few more locks. "*Doctah* Kang *wuz* sure *Moksanim wuz* keeping money *fwum duh* school *constwuction* budget. He said he *had-ah pwoof* in his *note-ah-book* but nobody *evah* saw it.

You *talkee* to *Pak Samonim*, she tell you...but maybe not, *that-sa* why you *talkee* to me, *wight Bwand?"*

"I'm just here for a haircut," Carter said innocently, like he had just been caught stealing a lollipop from her kiddy bowl.

"You a big *liah, Bwand*, but you cute *liah."*

"*Anyang hasayo,*" she bid goodbye as the last customer exited the salon. "OK, we *talkee* now. *Moksanim* bought house this year, *reewy* nice house. *Doctah* Kang said he *got-a duh* money *faw duh* house *fwum duh kick-a downs."*

"Kickbacks?" Carter corrected again.

"*WHATEVAH!* You find that *note-ah-book* and maybe you find *killah."*

Jane held a mirror behind Carter's head to give him a full view of his haircut. "Masterful, as usual, Jane. You're more than a hairstylist, you're an artist, a poet with clippers," he said, and slipped a ten dollar tip into her apron.

"And you *buhrshit ahtist, Bwand,*" Jane said while struggling very briefly and unsuccessfully to return the tip.

CHAPTER 24 CHOI

"PLEASE MAKE yourself comfortable," Pastor Choi said. "Let me take your coat. Can I get you Something to drink? I have just made some coffee."

"No thank you, *Moksanim*," Carter said, and sat down on the leather sofa in the living room in Reverend Choi's parsonage.

"I won't take much of your time, Reverend. Thank you for seeing me."

"Oh, anytime. I always enjoy our conversations," said the pastor seated in a chair opposite Carter. He leaned forward. "I'm not sure how much more information I can provide, though. Kang Sangwoo was a strong member of Gethsemane Church. His death was a shock to all of us."

"*Moksanim*, Reverend Choi," Carter started again, not wanting to sound overly patronizing, "do you have any idea what Dr. Kang was so upset about at the service several weeks ago?"

Choi pulled off his glasses and rubbed his eyes. His face looked tired now. "Inspector Brand," he continued more formally now to match his weary look, "we tried. God knows how much we tried to get him to cooperate. He would not listen to reason; so thick necked. He just kept spreading lies and rumors about me and the elders calling us thieves, degenerates and criminals. We were about to have him expelled from Gethsemane when we heard of his murder."

This was disturbing new information. How could he have gone so long without discovering what everyone but he seemed to know? Was it his blind obsession with Jeannie Park-Reed or respect for Pastor Choi that delayed this obvious interview? The game had now changed. From Choi's disclosure, Carter found motive for Kang's murder but no obvious suspect. He needed to speak with the elders.

"*Moksanim*, I will have that cup of coffee if the offer is still good."

"Of course, it will be my pleasure. Just one minute," the pastor said, and disappeared into the kitchen. "Do you take sugar?" he called out.

"Just milk is fine," Carter shouted back.

Choi's single-story bungalow's living room was compact and unusually laid out as if the furniture collectively drew focus to the darkened hallway leading to the bedroom. Several months back, Carter had only grudgingly accepted the Blackberry phone issued to him by the department regarding it, at the time, as a high-tech leash. But at that moment, he found utility in the phone's built-in camera and discretely snapped a few frames of the highly polished hardwood floor. Pastor Choi returned with the coffee as Carter stuffed the Blackberry into its holster in his breast pocket.

"How long had Dr. Kang been a member of Gethsemane?" Carter asked after the pastor returned to his chair.

103

"Hmm, let me see. It was shortly before Pastor Reed was hired as the youth pastor. About three years ago, I recall."

"When did he start causing trouble?"

"Just after we broke ground on the new school. Dr. Kang began accusing me and the elders of mishandling the money, mismanaging the project and anything else he could think of. We had an outside accounting firm do a complete audit and they found nothing improper. We thought that would settle things but he continued; he just would not stop. That's when it became clear that he had other ideas - how should I say it? - a private agenda."

Carter took a final sip of coffee and put the cup down on the table. He rose to leave. "*Moksanim*, thank you for taking time out of your busy schedule to speak with me today. Your help is much appreciated. Can I ask a favor?"

"Of course, Inspector, what can I do for you?"

"You mentioned an independent audit. Would you mind terribly if I obtained a copy of that report?"

"It would be my pleasure. I will have Mrs. Park send one over to you tomorrow."

With that, Carter put on his shoes, shook Reverend Choi's hand and left.

CHAPTER 25 LOVE LETTERS

"WE JUST GOT this package messengered from your ladyfriend at Gethsemane," said Jason, presenting Carter with a thick, letter-size, manila envelope. "It's probably the audit you were waiting for."

"That was quick."

"Also, we have translated copies of letters we found on Kang's office computer. They were to a Soo-Ji Kim. It's possible that the Suzy we're looking for is Soo-Ji anglicized. And one more thing, we found calls to an S. Kim in the AT&T report on Kang's phone activity. It might be Suzy but Kim is the most common Korean surname so it could be from anyone." Carter read the letter.

> *My Dearest Soo-Ji,*
>
> *Through his limitless grace and wisdom, Father God has miraculously brought us together. Who else but I knows the pain you have suffered and what you have gone through? But your days of fear and loneliness will soon be over, my darling. I am here to take care of you and love you forever as only I can.*
>
> *My undying love and devotion,*
>
> *Kang*

"A love letter? Kang was desperately in love with this Soo-Ji? Is she the mysterious Suzy? And if she is, why the hell would she want to kill him?" Carter wondered aloud.

"Maybe the answer is in this next letter," Jason said, and handed Carter a second sheet.

Soo-Ji (or should I call you Suzy again?),

You know how sorry I always felt for you and what you needed to do to make a life for yourself when we were in college. Every hour with you would bring me such joy and I swore that some day I would take you away from that life and make you a respectable woman. I found out about your visits to Choi. Do you still need money so badly that you would condemn your eternal soul to hell? I won't give up on you, Soo-Ji! I know that buried in your heart is the soul of a righteous woman who can be saved through the blood of Christ but I can't let this sin continue. I love you and will do anything necessary to save you for your own good.

Your shining knight,

Kang

Carter spit cold coffee back into the cup on his desk that had become a Petri dish of hairy mold. "Bleh," he revulsed.

"So, we go on the assumption that this Soo-Ji is the same Suzy who contacted Benezek?" Jason asked Carter, who was still clearing the taste of rancid brew from his mouth.

"We need to find this Suzy or Soo-Ji. Maybe then we can find a stronger motive than harassment. He indicated in his letter that they knew each other in college. Let's take another look at Kang's condo."

CHAPTER 26 BETWEEN THE BOOKS

THE ENTRANCE to Kang's twelfth floor condominium was still secured with crisscrossed yellow crime scene tape forcing Carter and Jason to squeeze through the open triangles. On the first visit they had done a basic search of the bedroom and office but, with the exception of Kang's password-protected computer, had left everything in place.

They were searching for the notebook that Kang insisted contained incriminating evidence against Choi. They started in the office with its five ceiling-high bookshelves crammed with a combination of medical journals, text books and books of classic art.

"I think we need to look at each book individually," Carter said. "The notebook could be anywhere between these books."

Jason understood, but was not pleased with the prospect of spending the afternoon combing through hundreds of hardcover books, paperbacks and magazines. Resigning himself to the task at hand, he pulled each volume off its shelf, one-by-one, shook it, and rudely tossed it on the floor when the object of their search was not revealed. Between a copy of <u>Sushruta Samhita</u> and <u>The Science of</u>

Beauty, Jason found what they were looking for. It was a collection of handwritten and laser printed sheets of paper, not a notebook, in a clear plastic binder. He removed them individually and laid them on the floor snapping a picture of each with the Blackberry camera.

The top sheet was a spreadsheet with monthly transaction details of the Gethsemane general fund bank account. Kang had circled in red eight $1000 withdrawals from a cash machine in a nearby convenience store. Checking the dates on his Blackberry, he noticed they occurred every other Wednesday over a four month period.

The next sheet was a copy of a letter from T. DiGiorno at Revelation Construction to Reverend Choi:

Dear Pastor Choi,

It was a pleasure meeting with you last week. As per our conversation we will deliver the surplus flooring from the gymnasium to your parsonage at the agreed upon date and time. Our humble appreciation for your continued patronage.

T.Giordano
Revelation Construction

The last page was from the IRS to Reverend Choi informing him of a thirty-thousand dollar personal tax liability.

Carter's head began to throb. He had always regarded Reverend Choi as a man of great wisdom and integrity and, despite the language barrier, came away from Choi's sermons inspired. Kang's documents considered alone without any clear context provided the motive for crimes of embezzlement and bribery, but would the fear of those crimes being discovered compel Choi to commit murder?

Carter had to find out if, in fact, crimes were committed by Choi or an associate.

He was puzzled. "How could Choi owe money to the IRS?" he asked Jason. "Isn't he exempt as an ordained minister?"

"I actually know this. Some pastors are paid on a 1099 so no taxes are withheld. Most are not great money managers and don't adequately put money aside each quarter for the government."

"Maybe the regular cash withdrawals were for tax bills?"

They continued examining each book on the shelves until Jason discovered a UCLA college yearbook. Inside, would they find Soo-Ji's picture and the social connection between her and Kang? They gathered the papers together and placed them back in the folder taking with them the folder and yearbook leaving a mountain of publications piled on the condo floor.

CHAPTER 27 THE LATE MR. DIGIORNO

THEY WERE on the way back to the precinct a few minutes after nine PM when Carter's Blackberry squawked the alert reserved only for emergency calls:

FROM: MPLSSRV03

TO: INSP. BRAND

SUBJ: 10-54d

INVESTIGATE REPORT OF BODY W. LAKE ST. 11-98 KOBINSKI

"I've had this phone for over a month now and I thought I knew how it worked, at least how all the important functions worked. I deleted this message to investigate a body by Lake Calhoun weeks ago when they found Kang and I just got it again," Carter said, and administered a firm smack of adjustment to the device.

"Let me see," said Jason sitting in the front passenger's seat. "This is a new message, boss. It's got today's date. I'll call in to confirm." Jason dialed the dispatcher. "It's not a mistake. We've got another body at Lake Calhoun." He reached over to switch on the dashboard beacon light. Carter pressed the reply button on the Blackberry to acknowledge the call and hit the siren.

Driving past a picnicking area across from Lake Calhoun they spotted a late model Cadillac off the side of the road several hundred yards in front of them. Carter pulled up behind it. Officer Kobinski stood guard as Dr. Ostrow and an assistant prepared to examine a body slumped forward in the font seat of the Cadillac. Jason began snapping pictures of the scene while Carter debriefed Kobinski.

"The engine was still running when we got here about an hour ago. We saw someone in the car and he wasn't moving. Figured he might be trying to commit suicide, or something, so we opened the driver side door. That's when we saw the gunshot wound on the side of his head and blood all over the seat. We called for an ambulance but they pronounced him dead right here. Then we called you and Strow."

"You ran the plates, right?"

"Yeah, forgot to mention. The vehicle is registered to a Thomas DiGiorno who lives - or should I say lived - in St. Paul."

Carter stretched his hands into a pair of latex gloves and opened the Cadillac's front passenger door. He shined his MagLite towards the driver's seat. The body was slumped over the steering wheel, arms hanging. The white interior headliner glowed red from a large, shimmering pool of blood on the carpet reflecting the flashlight beam as Carter angled the light towards the floor in front of the passenger seat. He called Jason over.

"Take pictures of this, son. He was shot in the head from the right, probably over here by the window judging from all the blood on this side. Somehow, he made it over the center console and into the driver's seat. Does that make any sense to you? The passenger side window isn't broken and the window is rolled down which tells me the shooter shot him from outside the passenger door. These are electric windows so the stiff must have opened the window from the driver's seat to talk to the person who shot him."

"Right, it doesn't make much sense that the dead guy did too much moving around with a gushing hole in his temple," Jason added. "Maybe the shooter moved him behind the wheel afterwards?"

Carter considered the possibility. "Or maybe he was behind the wheel when he was shot and then moved over to the passenger seat to allow the shooter, or someone with the shooter, to drive the car to Lake Calhoun."

"You're thinking he wasn't shot here?"

"That's what I'm thinking."

Carter tossed Jason a pair of latex gloves. "He's all yours, Strow. Before you take him away, let the sergeant look in his pockets."

Dr. Ostrow and his assistant slowly lifted the body out of the driver's seat and onto a low gurney. It was fully dressed in the pants and vest of a brown three-piece suit. The jacket was hanging from a hook between the front and back doors. Jason found only a pack of cigarettes in the vest pockets. He reached over the front seat and removed a wallet from the suit jacket's left inner pocket. From the right outer pocket he found a cell phone. He showed it to Carter.

"What the hell's this?"

"It's the dead guy's cell phone," Jason said.

"Where are all the buttons?"

"It's an iPhone. It doesn't have buttons, just this touch screen."

"Well, touch it and see who he's been calling."

Jason traced his finger over the phone's display until he discovered the button that listed outgoing calls. "Boss, he made calls to Choi's home four times in the last two days."

"Anything in there that might indicate where he was today?"

"There's probably a calendar in here somewhere." After more frantic finger swiping, Jason said, "Ah, there it is, found it. Let's see. He had an appointment to meet Choi at Gethsemane about four hours ago."

He deposited both items found on DiGiorno's person in a zip-lock evidence bag. Inside the car, he located and pushed the button to open the trunk where he found samples of floor tile and a black briefcase which he took to their car along with the other evidence they had collected.

"We're through here," Carter said to Kobinski, and waved to Dr. Ostrow that he could leave with the body.

Carter had not been concerned with media exposure after Kang's murder. The story hadn't made better than page five in *The Tribune* and was completely ignored by the local TV and cable channels. This covert racism was just fine with the Korean community that was never comfortable with Caucasian involvement in their private affairs anyway. Carter figured he was accepted at Gethsemane only because he was socially regarded as Hannah's guest rather than a bona fide member of the church. When the news of DiGiorno's murder got out - a white man's murder at the same location - Carter knew that shielding the church from a media onslaught would be impossible.

He was right. The Fifth Precinct front parking lot was awash with ponds of arc light illuminating an army of reporters itching to shove a microphone in the face of anyone who might have information on what would now be known as "The Calhoun Serial Murders". News vans with their telescoping microwave Asherah poles cluttered the lot and side streets.

Carter and Jason drove past the media crowd and into the precinct parking deck. They grabbed the evidence bags and went directly to the video room where they clicked-on the local cable channel on the big wall monitor. On the screen was Captain Cohen, bathed in bright light, on the precinct steps with a video border reading "BREAKING STORY: CALHOUN KILLER STRIKES AGAIN", deflecting questions shouted at him by the rabid reporters:

"Do you have any leads?"

"Do you have any evidence that the murders are related?"

"Do you have any suspects?"

"Is Lake Calhoun Park safe?"

"Folks, we will provide information as the facts are learned. The investigation is ongoing and I can't comment or speculate on the details. Right now our thoughts and prayers should be with the families of the deceased," Cohen said and turned to enter the precinct house with the mob of reporters still shouting questions at his back.

"Brand!" Captain Cohen yelled immediately upon reentering the building. "Where is Inspector Brand?" he bellowed to no one in particular. A uniformed officer pointed towards the ceiling.

"Tell Inspector Brand I want to see him in my office immediately," Cohen said and slammed his office door behind him.

Two minutes later, Carter opened his Captain's office door just far enough to stick his head inside.

"You wanted to see me, Captain?"

"Get in here, sit down and close the door." Carter complied quickly, leaving Jason outside the office door, pacing. "We need to close this case right away, Carter. You can count on non-stop scrutiny and pressure from the media jackals. They'll whip the public into a frenzy and drive us nuts. Where do we stand with the first murder, what's his name, Kang?"

"Well, there are several people of interest but..."

"But nothing, Carter. Who do you like the most? Who is your lead suspect?"

"Well, Captain, we're still waiting for the ballistics. After Strow digs out the slug from tonight's victim, we can run tests on it to see if it was the same shooter."

"We don't have that much time. I want an update on my desk by tomorrow with your suspects and evidence compiled so far. I want that report by tomorrow evening."

CHAPTER 28 EVIDENCE

CARTER FELT the vise jaws of the case squeezing tighter. He needed to reexamine all the evidence collected to date: interview transcripts, fingerprints, ballistics reports, phone records and the impounded physical items. As cases go, there were not a lot of items related to the Kang case in the evidence room: three cell phones in small zip-lock bags labeled "Kang", "Benezek" and "female"; Kang's home and office computers; three twenty-dram vials of pills, also in separate zip-lock bags; Kang's clothing; the folder with Kang's letters, and the keys from Kang's SUV fastened together on a fob from Weinberg's stationery store.

Weinberg's:

-The mega stationery store that dates back to the nineteenth century.

-The family-run business that managed to survive brutal competition from the national discount stationery chains.

-Where one Calvin Chennault pilfered an expensive pen and became an entry in a Minneapolis criminal database.

Carter signed out the keys.

CHAPTER 29 CALVIN II

JASON ESCORTED Chennault into the corner office where Carter was sitting at his desk waiting for them. He dangled the bagged set of keys at eye level.

"Welcome back, Calvin," Carter said with a singsong greeting. "Recognize these?"

The young man took a seat in front of the desk, put his feet up on the desktop and quickly examined the keys through the zip-lock bag. "Appears to be a set of keys," he answered, stoically.

"Anything special about those keys?"

"Because they're the keys to the SUV you picked me up in?" Calvin inquired, underscoring the obvious.

"And how is it, Calvin, that you recognize the keys from the SUV after having them in your possession so briefly?"

Calvin smirked and looked away. "I guess the Weinberg's logo kinda jogged my memory."

"That's right, Weinberg's. Look at me young man. That's the same store with which you have some history, if my fifty-one year-old memory serves me correctly."

117

Chennault rolled his eyes. "So this is why I'm back here? Your fifty-one year-old brain put two and two together and concluded an old stationery store ties me to the murder?"

"Don't you find it an odd coincidence that your only previous crime was at the store whose logo is on the dead man's key fob that we found in the dead man's car being driven by you?"

Calvin picked up the bag and took a closer look at the keys. He tossed it back to the desktop. "Not really, and that ain't a key fob."

Carter picked it up and straightened his glasses. "OK, so it's not a fob, not that it matters." He looked at Calvin over his glasses. "So what is it, then?"

Calvin snatched the bag and through the plastic worked a cap off the top of the fob revealing a stubby, metal connector. "It's a memory stick."

Jason examined the device through the bag. "You stick it in a USB port on your computer and you can store files in it. You use it to take files with you," Jason explained.

"So, I can go?" Calvin asked, now on his feet and leaning towards the door.

"What? Yeah, fine, thanks for coming in, Calvin," Carter said, dismissing him without taking his eyes off the memory stick. Jason had already located a USB port on the back of Carter's computer which gave the tell-tale *bing-bong* as he inserted the memory stick into it. A window on the display opened presenting icons of different file types all titled with unreadable square symbols.

"The file names are probably in Korean," Jason said and placed his MacBook laptop computer on the desk. He flipped it open, unplugged the memory stick from Carter's PC and plugged it into his Apple laptop launching a window containing the file icons with the file names in geometric *hangul* characters. "This one," Jason said. "sooji.mov - it's a video."

Jason double-clicked the icon. A QuickTime viewer presented a rectangular window about the size of an index card. Jason clicked the play button to start the video.

First to appear in the video was a date displayed in the upper right in mm/dd/yyyy format, 8:22 PM. It was the day of Kang's murder. After a few seconds, the date disappeared and the action quickly cut to a desaturated, bouncing view of the front door of a house dimly lit by a single porch light.

The video zoomed to the house number, 40, and lingered there for a few moments before moving left. The video stopped then resumed suddenly with the focus on a rear window illuminated by a single lamp from within. Slowly, the frame lifted to the window, paused, and then raised more until the bedroom came into view. Through open slats of Venetian blinds, the grainy video showed the vertical harmonic motion of a woman's lower torso, her blouse and skirt intact.

"Kang was a goddamned peeper?" Jason blurted, more out of amusement than astonishment.

Carter remained silent, rapt in concentration on the still-playing video. Jason glanced over at his partner, puzzled at his continued interest in a video that appeared to have no relevance to the case.

"Boss?" Jason interrupted. Carter remained glued to the video. "Carter?" Jason asked quietly, sensing there was more to the video than was obvious to him. Carter continued watching.

Shame's Evidence

The woman's body stopped its up and down movement and for the briefest moment her face, in profile, dipped into view then back behind the shield of the blinds. Carter and Jason watched as she removed a condom from her prone partner and turned off the light as she left the room clutching her bag. As the video ended Carter buried his face in his hands.

The woman's face was not visible long enough to be easily identified and it didn't really matter. Carter could have the frame of the video enhanced and enlarged to see if it matched any mug shots of hookers that might be in the system. But he knew the house. His hands wiped to the sides of his face and as his eyes emerged he knew he was in a different world; one where anger, logic, passion, hate and despair gripped equally at his viscera leaving him a nauseous and confused excuse for a man.

CHAPTER 30 MOKSANIM EXPLAINS

CARTER KNOCKED on Choi's office door at Gethsemane Church. *"Cham kan munyo!"* the pastor called out to acknowledge the knock and request the caller to wait. A few moments later, he opened the door.

"Inspector Brand, Carter, please come in," Pastor Choi said, surprised that Carter had come by without notice.

Carter closed the door behind him and took a seat on the guest couch. Choi sat on an upholstered chair opposite him, a mahogany coffee table between them.

"Moksanim, can we talk privately?"

"Of course. What can I help you with today?" Choi said, and moved to lock the office door.

Carter began respectfully. "Pastor, while investigating the murder of Dr. Kang we have discovered certain items that are quite, well, troubling."

Choi leaned closer. "Please, go on."

"Moksanim, since I have known you for a number of years and very much admire you and respect you, I felt you deserved a chance to respond directly...privately."

Carter set Jason's laptop computer on the coffee table and flipped open the cover. While it booted, he rotated it to give Choi a better angle. Then he pulled Kang's folder out of the laptop's case and placed it on the coffee table next to the computer. Choi's expression stiffened.

"Dr. Kang had in his possession bank statements from a church account with regular withdrawals from an ATM in a liquor store near here. I spoke with the owner who remembers seeing you."

Choi positioned his glasses. "Yes, I buy *soju* from Jimmy Shin's store on occasion – more frequently since my wife passed away, I'm afraid – but I do not take money from the cash machine. In fact, I could not even tell you where the bank card is. In financial matters I am quite helpless, I must confess."

"He also had a copy of a letter from the Internal Revenue Service notifying you of a substantial tax liability."

The pastor responded quickly. "Yes, another one of my oversights. I am taking care of that matter with an accountant."

"*Moksanim*, the hardwood flooring in your house matches the flooring in the new Gethsemane gymnasium."

"Yes, when I purchased this house the floor was in terrible condition. For the repairs, Mrs. Park suggested I use the same contractor who built the gym floor because I could get a special discount."

Carter shook his head. "Reverend, I know you had the best of intentions, and your naiveté is genuine, but don't you see how the conflict of interest might raise suspicions? And the fact that the salesman from the company was just

murdered makes the situation even more suspicious. Can't
you see that?"

"Carter, I am a simple man. My life is dedicated to
serving God and the people of God."

Carter double-clicked the movie icon on the laptop
computer. Leaning closer, Choi watched the video action
move to the front door and the house number, close-up,
verifying what he feared. Sparing Choi pointless torture,
Carter let the video run for only a few moments until it
reached the point where only the woman's lower half could
be seen in the bedroom. The pastor buried his face in his
hands and wept softly.

Carter put his hand on Choi's shoulder. "*Moksanim*, I
know you to be a good and honorable man, but you are still
a man. I could never blame you for seeking the pleasure of a
woman after losing your wife. Everyone knows how dearly
you loved her. But if you paid for call girl appointments with
church money it's a serious problem."

Choi looked up at Carter like he was seeing him
through a kaleidoscope. "What? Is that what you think? I am
stealing from the church to pay for prostitutes? Carter, I am
a man, a flawed man, who accepts all his failings and
weaknesses. But I am a forgiven man, too. Gethsemane
compensates me generously for my work and I have no need
to steal from the offering plate. On occasion, I do seek the
pleasure of a woman so that I might remember the only
woman I ever loved. Can you not understand that?"

"Frankly, I do not know what to believe or even think
right now. You are a very special person who has been there
for me in my own time of loneliness. Reverend, I am a
homicide detective and two men with ties to Gethsemane
have been murdered. Engaging the services of prostitutes is a

crime. While not a felony, it forces me to question your judgment with more serious matters."

"Please, Inspector, spare me your Sunday School epiphanies. What I did I did with full knowledge of the consequences. I am no longer a married man and it will be up to The Lord to decide my eternal fate, not you or anyone else.

Choi's words no longer had meaning; no more legitimate than the mad ravings of a park bench lunatic. Carter closed the laptop's cover without bothering to shut it down. "I will be back, Reverend. We have more to discuss."

CHAPTER 31 FILES

CARTER WAITED UNTIL all the downstairs lights in the church had been extinguished and the last worshippers had drifted out to their cars before giving his team of detectives the order to move. Jason led them to the finance office in the basement where he found Elder Kwon sitting at his desk.

Spoken in Korean, Jason identified himself and served the warrant to seize Gethsemane documents. The Elder responded calmly. "Sergeant, I would prefer we keep our conversation in English so that there is no misunderstanding with your men."

"Mr. Kwon, we are hear to serve a warrant allowing us to search and seize any and all files relating to Gethsemane Church finances in this office. Will you allow the warrant to be executed?"

"Do I have a choice?"

"It would make things easier all around if we did our work with your cooperation, sir."

Kwon pushed his swivel chair away from his desk. "You may proceed, Sergeant."

Two detectives searched the office and adjoining rooms for file cabinets and slapped yellow "EVIDENCE" stickers on each one they found. They were followed by two more detectives who carted the labeled cabinets away on rolling hand trucks. While pulling one of the trucks up a short flight of stairs, a cabinet fell off the truck's platform and crashed to the ground.

"I told you to be careful with those, you idiot!" Jason screamed. "Show some respect. You're in a church."

In all, thirteen file cabinets and five boxes of loose documents were collected and wheeled out of the office and into the waiting van.

CHAPTER 32 SOO-JI

THE IMAGE OF Seoul Metropolitan Police Agency Superintendent Joo-Chan Lee snapped into focus on the large flat screen monitor in the precinct Polycom room.

"Hello, hello? Can you hear me Minneapolis? We can see you."

Jason zoomed the camera out and hailed back, "*Anyang hasayo? Junun* Sergeant Kim *imnida.*"

"Good Morning, Sergeant. It would be rude to Inspector Brand if we did not conduct our discussion in English."

"Thank you, Superintendent," said Carter. "Your English is very good – much better than my Korean."

"Thank you, Inspector. I attended college in America, Princeton University. If you ever find yourself in Princeton, New Jersey, be sure to have lunch at Tony's sandwich shop. The trash can with hot peppers was my favorite."

"Thanks for the tip, Superintendent. I will keep that in mind."

"But I'm sure you did not wake up so early to hear my college nostalgia," Lee said as he adjusted his glasses and opened a manila folder on the table in front of him. "So, you want to know about the Hong Soo-Ji case"?

"Hong?" Carter interrupted. "We have been looking for a Soo-Ji Kim."

"She used Kim as an alias, we assume, to fade into the Korean population in America. Her real surname is Hong. It is an interesting case, one of my first after being promoted to SMPA Superintendent. I can send you the details by fax but I believe it is worth recounting the story now. Would you care to hear it? Do you have time?"

"We have enough time and coffee," Carter replied. "Would you mind if I start the recorder?"

"Not at all. Let me know when you are ready for me to start."

Jason slid a fresh tape into the VCR, pressed the record button and signaled for Lee to begin. Lee held a black & white, 8 x 10 inch photograph of a young girl in front of the camera. She looked to be about 17 or 18, dark black hair set in a pony tail, plain, black-rimmed glasses in front of her narrow eyes and a prominent bump on the bridge of her nose. Superintendent Lee began.

"Hong Soo-Ji lived in a comfortable apartment with her mother in the Bundang district of Seoul. She was the daughter of Hong Ho-Sun, a prosperous owner of a company that manufactures and exports women's garments. He took Soo-Ji's mother, Kim Sun-Ok, as his second wife."

"What happened to his first wife?" Carter asked.

"Inspector, in Korea, polygamy is still one of the shadow privileges of wealthy men. He never legally married Soo-Ji's mother but accepted responsibility for their livelihood and Soo-Ji's education. She was a good student and had been accepted at Seoul University when her father died suddenly in a car accident leaving nothing in his will for young Soo-Ji or her mother.

Their apartment's rent was quite costly and they were used to an opulent lifestyle. They owned a luxury car and threw frequent parties for Soo-Ji's father's society friends when he was alive.

After they ran out of money, her mother started an exclusive brothel in their apartment patronized by a select group of her late husband's business associates. One night, her late husband's sales manager, Lim Seung-Kyu, showed up without notice, quite drunk. He insisted on bedding young Soo-Ji and threatened to inform the police about her mother's enterprise if she refused. He argued and physically struggled with Soo-Ji's mother. When he struck her, Soo-Ji agreed to his request."

"Who related these events to you?" Carter interrupted.

"You're getting ahead of me, Inspector. I promise to answer your questions before you finish that coffee."

"I'm sorry, Superintendent, please continue."

"Lim was found dead in a trash dumpster behind her building three days later with knife wounds to his neck and abdomen. Meanwhile, Soo-Ji's mother sent her away to America to avoid arrest.

To answer your question, Inspector, Soo-Ji's mother had confessed to the murder and we found her fingerprints on the knife. After she was arrested, one of the regular girls in Soo-Ji's mother's employ told the story of Lim's arrival and identified Soo-Ji as the murderer. Her cooperation was part of a plea-bargain agreement to avoid being charged with prostitution. Even though there was no corroboration, a warrant was issued for Soo-Ji's arrest. About ten years ago we had information that she was working in a Los Angeles massage parlor but never located her and have had no word since. She just vanished into the local population."

"Thank you, Superintendent, this has been most helpful."

"Any time, Inspector, we are always pleased to assist our friends in American law enforcement. Please accept our open invitation to visit us in Seoul. Perhaps you and the sergeant might find the need for additional investigation here?"

"Thanks for the offer, Superintendent, perhaps one day."

"*Anyang hashimnika,*" Jason thanked the superintendent, bowed to the video camera and closed the video transmission.

CHAPTER 33 AUDIT

JASON RECRUITED two detectives from the fraud investigations squad to assist him in poring over the documents seized from Gethsemane. Stacks of papers occupied all but a few square inches of the conference room table around which the detectives worked with unopened boxes on one side, emptied boxes on the other.

"Jason, how many members did you figure Gethsemane church has now?" asked detective Steve Kaufman.

"Inspector Brand's been doing an informal count on Sundays for the past couple of weeks. I think they've been averaging about four hundred a Sunday."

Kaufman selected a document from a stack labeled "MEMBERS." "Well, I just counted the membership registrations from two months ago and I got about seven-fifty. If you look at the weekly cash offerings they've declined steadily since then. During that same period the funds drawn from the church endowment fund rose at about the same rate the offerings were declining."

"To compensate for the shortfall, no doubt," Jason said.

"Clearly," Kaufman agreed and leafed through another folder. "Well, this is interesting: the amount of money kicked up to the national church remained constant. Shouldn't that amount vary with the number of church members?"

"As far as I know. Maybe they were paying based on the actual number of registered members, not on the ones who actually show up. Maybe the ones who defected to another church never cancelled their membership."

"But why would they want to prop up the membership numbers if money was getting tight?" Kaufman asked.

"Good question. We need to take a trip to the other big Korean church around here, Hope Presbyterian, to see how many Gethsemane members might have joined the exodus and worship there."

CHAPTER 34 HOPE

WAITING ON THE front stoop outside of the attractive Windom Park parsonage, Pastor Tak Oh Chun's wife, Ji-Yai Im greeted Carter and Jason.

"*Anyang hasayo,*" they exchanged simultaneously. Inside, the Pastor approached the open door to shake their hands.

"Gentlemen, please come in," the pastor said. "May I get you some tea or a soft drink?"

After removing their shoes, Carter and Jason took seats on the sofa. "No, thank you, Reverend, we're good."

Carter began the meeting. "*Moksanim,* as I mentioned on the telephone, we are investigating the murder of Dr. Sangwoo Kang who was a prominent member of Gethsemane church. We understand there had been a controversy at Gethsemane involving the senior pastor and the church elders which led to a number of members leaving for Hope. We are not looking for names, but if it would not be too much trouble, we would like to know the number and dates of Gethsemane members who have transferred their official church membership to Hope."

"Yes, Inspector, you mentioned that on the phone and I have the figures you are looking for. I think a good number of Gethsemane members attend here regularly but have not officially transferred their membership, probably hoping to return to Gethsemane after things settle down there."

"You don't mind that?" Carter asked.

"No, not really. Our membership is growing well independently of the disaffected Gethsemane members. They tithe well and are made to feel at home by our membership so, no, we do not mind at all. I have included on this sheet a column of the number of Gethsemane 'visitors' we see regularly."

Pastor Chun handed Carter a manila envelope containing a neatly laid-out spreadsheet with columns labeled GETHSEMANE MEMBER and GETHSEMANE VISITOR with dates at each intersecting row.

Carter accepted the document and rose to leave. "Thank, you, Reverend, this is very helpful. We appreciate your time," he said while shaking the Pastor's hand.

Before Carter and Jason could leave, the pastor's *samonim* appeared carrying a tray with three glasses of a brass-colored liquid. "Please, gentlemen, you must have some *bori cha* before leaving" she said while offering glasses to the men.

"*Kamsa hamnida,*" Jason thanked.

"Have you ever tasted barley tea?" she asked Carter.

"Yes, my wife would make it often."

"Oh, she is Asian?"

"Yes, she is Korean."

"And did you teach your children to speak Korean?" she asked.

"We are still childless," Carter replied, politely.

The pastor frowned, embarrassed at his wife's indiscretion. "Please forgive my wife, Inspector, she did not mean to intrude."

"Not a problem, *Moksanim*, perhaps one day I will be blessed with children as well." They finished the tea, thanked the pastor and his wife for their help and hospitality, put on their shoes and left.

CHAPTER 35 HIPAA

JASON BURST INTO Carter's office. "Boss, Kang's medical records were just impounded! I didn't have a chance to go through them."

"What!"

"Two guys from the Sheriff's office just carted away all twelve boxes," Jason answered breathlessly.

"On whose authority?"

"The H.C.S.O. deputies had a warrant from a Hennepin County Judge, Kathryn Prentiss. It said the records were protected by H.I.P.A.A. That's the Health Insuran..."

"I know what the fucking HIPAA act is, dammit! She was way outside her authority – at least I think she was," Carter screamed. "You mind the fort. I'm going to Sixth Street to pay Ms. Prentiss a call." He grabbed his jacket and cane and limped out of his office.

Thirty minutes later, Carter hobbled out of the elevator and down the hall to the office of Civil Court Judge Kathryn Prentiss. "Inspector Brand to see Judge Prentiss," Carter said to the young, bubble gum-snapping receptionist. She continued tweeting text into her cell phone, self-amused, without acknowledging his presence. Carter displayed his badge inches from the girl's nose. "Would you please inform the Judge that I am here?" Carter insisted, annoyed.

Equally annoyed at the interruption of her thought train, she looked up and asked, "Do you have an appointment?"

"No!"

"Well, she's not here. You'll have to wait."

Carter turned towards a nearby empty chair in the waiting area coming face-to-face with Judge Prentiss, the key to her office door in hand.

"What happened to you?" she asked coolly upon seeing Carter's cane.

"I guess I worked out a bit too long on the Stair Master."

"Charlene, please hold my calls," she said while entering her office with Carter following. The receptionist did not respond having resumed her furious cell phone textation. "Charlene!" the judge yelled.

Carter followed the judge into her office and closed the door. "Have a seat Inspector. If you're looking for me to abrogate my injunction on inspecting those medical records the answer is no."

"The way I read HIPAA, Your Honor, we are allowed to examine medical records without patient consent if the information contained therein is needed to identify or locate a suspect, fugitive, material witness, or missing person. We believe the particulars of the Kang case meet that criterion," Carter appealed, reading off notes scribbled on a coffee-stained napkin.

"Oh? And are you now practicing law, Brand? How about leaving interpretation of the law to me and you concentrate on catching bad guys, OK?"

"That's what I am trying to do, your honor, but you're making my job very difficult."

The judge shot straight up. "Don't try my patience, Brand. You're fishing in dangerous waters. More than a few of Kang's patients called this office to make sure that their before-and-after pictures did not end up on one of your gorillas' Flickr pages. I'm more interested in protecting their rights than giving you an easy shortcut. If you don't have any better justification for violating a patient's privacy you can stop wasting my time and get the hell out of here!" She bellowed her words pointing to the door.

Carter paused while the judge regained her composure. "Kathryn, you know I would not have come here if it wasn't absolutely necessary to examine those records. Please don't make this any more difficult than it has to be."

Judge Prentiss sat back down. "Go to hell, Brand. Don't try to make this about us. We both moved on a long time ago. Are you still good at moving on, Carter? Maybe you should forget about the records and move on with your case," she said, bitterly.

"Kathryn, please. You won't have to worry about the confidentiality of the records, I personally guarantee it."

"Right. You never worried too much about hurting people who cared for you so why should I believe that you or your juvenile cronies would respect the rights of complete strangers?" Prentiss seemed to choke back tears.

Carter exhaled. "You're right, I have been selfish and insensitive in my personal life - maybe still am – but I am still a professional sworn to protect the public. That is a commitment I hold above all else. I'm a good cop, Kathryn, you can trust me."

She glanced at him skeptically and picked up the phone. "Get out of here, Carter. I'll let you know."

"Thank you, Your Honor," he said, and left the office.

CHAPTER 36 PARABELLUM

JASON TURNED from the water cooler as Carter hobbled past on the way to his office. "You must have really turned on the charm, boss."

"Excuse me?"

"The Sherriff's guys just brought back the boxes of Kang's records."

Carter shook his head and smiled. "It must have been my honest face."

"We finally got the ballistics report on the slug they pulled out of Kang: nine millimeter parabellum with rifling marks that suggest a Baretta M9, the NATO standard. It also matched the bullet that killed the salesman."

"Did you check our suspects lists for registered handguns?"

Jason turned reticent while thumbing through the pages of the report. Carter waited a few minutes before asking again, "Did you hear me?"

"Yes, boss, we got one hit when I did a database search cross referencing registered nine millimeter gun owners with the names of our suspects. Now that we have the names of Kang's patients we need to check them as well."

"Fine, so whose name came up?"

Jason looked at Carter. "It was Choi *Moksanim*. He has owned an M9 for almost fifteen years. He must have registered it voluntarily."

Carter's gut tensed. He remembered Jeannie telling him that Choi had been a chaplain in the Korean army before immigrating to the United States. Might he have held onto his old officer's sidearm? He had motive to kill Kang who was actively working to remove him from the church. And Kang's agitation was dividing the membership prompting many families to flee Gethsemane for Hope Church taking their tithes with them.

They needed to get that gun and to do that needed a warrant to search Pastor Choi's parsonage. Carter dialed Judge Prentiss.

CHAPTER 37 RIGHT TO BEAR ARMS

JASON STAYED BEHIND in the Prius while Carter knocked on the door at forty Washburn Place. Though it was still early evening, not quite eight, Pastor Choi opened the door already dressed in pajamas and robe.

"I apologize for the late visit, *Moksanim*, but I wanted to handle this business personally. May I come in?"

"Of course, Carter, and I apologize for my evening attire."

Carter left his shoes at the front door which under normal circumstances would have been standard practice when entering a Korean home. This was not a social call, however, so the appropriateness of removing his shoes gave him pause.

"*Moksanim*, the purpose of my visit relates directly to the Kang case. We've determined that he was shot with a nine millimeter pistol, probably of the type used by the military. The records show that there is a handgun of that type registered to you. Is it still in your possession?"

"Yes, Inspector, I still have it but I have not even looked at it for over ten years," Choi said, and immediately started down the hall to his bedroom. Carter followed.

"It has more sentimental than practical value, really. The automatic pistol was presented to me by the Commanding General of the Third South Korean Army upon my discharge as a chaplain. It is just a keepsake, really."

In the bedroom, Choi reached under his bed and slid out a square aluminum case engraved with *hangul* lettering and the *Yin/Yang* symbol of the Republic of Korea flag. Choi laid it on top of the bed, dug out the key from his top desk drawer and unlocked it, snapping open the left lock then the right. He opened the case and removed a dark chamois cloth exposing the shiny weapon. Holding the cover open, he looked at Carter for acknowledgement that he had revealed everything without resistance.

"Thank you for being so cooperative about this matter, *Moksanim*. Would you mind if I borrowed this for a little while?"

Choi frowned and kept his hand on the gun case. "Inspector Brand, while I have the greatest respect for you, I am wondering if consulting an attorney at this point might be the most prudent thing for me to do. Lately, my ignorance has resulted in unfortunate situations."

"That is your right, Reverend, but I will need to take the weapon with me now."

Choi closed the cover. "I assume you have proper authorization?"

"Yes. I did not serve it because I knew I could count on your cooperation."

Choi handed Carter the case. "I have nothing to hide - you may take the gun. Please make sure it is not damaged and that it is eventually returned. It has great sentimental value to me."

CHAPTER 38 WEAPON

CARTER APPREHENSIVELY slid out the single 8½ x 11 inch ballistics report from the manila envelope. His eyes scanned past the descriptive information, the procedural notes and the testing data stopping short on the only word in the entire report that held any meaning for him: MATCH.

He pulled his palms down over his face from eyes to chin. Choi had motive and the murder weapon, but did he have opportunity? The first frame of the cell phone video of his sex episode displayed the time and date - the same date as Kang's murder. The officially recorded time-of-death was only a coroner's estimation. Carter needed to find out Choi's whereabouts for that entire evening; it would be his only alibi. He grabbed the Prius keys.

With Jason following one step behind, Carter grasped the iron banister of Pastor Choi's brick front steps and took each painful step slowly; physically painful from the parking garage fight with Perry Johnson and emotionally painful from the knowledge that with each step he might be that much closer to putting his pastor under arrest for murder.

He twisted the pitted brass doorbell knob. It made no sound. He brought his knuckles to the door just as Choi pulled it open.

"Good afternoon, gentlemen, please come in. I trust this visit brings good news?"

"Let's sit down, *Moksanim*," Carter said, directing the pastor to a dining room chair. "There has been a very serious development. The bullet that killed Dr. Kang was fired from your handgun. The test results were conclusive."

"But that is impossible! The pistol case is locked and only I have the key. Certainly, you don't suspect me."

"I am in a very difficult position. Knowing you for so long and knowing the man you are my inclination is to believe you. But *Moksanim*, the evidence is overwhelming against you. Sergeant Kim is going to show you the video again and, as painful as it might be to watch, you need to be completely truthful with us."

Jason setup his MacBook on the dining room table and double clicked the icon to start the grainy video playing.

"Haven't we been through this, Inspector? Did you come here to torture me?"

Jason explained to the pastor. "*Moksanim*, the date on the video is the date of Dr. Kang's murder. The time of his death is just a coroner's estimate. This video proves that you were occupied at about the same time Kang was killed. If we could account more specifically for your time on that date it would provide you with an alibi. Can you give us any information about your visitor, how you made the appointment or what time she arrived and left?"

Distraught, Choi wrung his hands. "I don't know, I don't know. She always came about ten o'clock on Monday nights. I just called a number I found in a newspaper in a box outside Jimmy Shin's store. They always sent the same girl."

"I don't suppose you know the girl's name," Carter asked.

"No, no, it was not important."

Carter pressed harder. "Reverend Choi, it is very important that you give us some information to verify your whereabouts on that night. Don't you understand?"

"I'm sorry, Inspector, I have nothing to offer. You will just have to believe that I was here all night from about ten o'clock."

Carter looked at Jason, resigned to the inevitable. Jason reached for the handcuffs on his belt.

"That won't be necessary, Sergeant," Carter said, blocking Jason's hand. He turned to Choi and said solemnly, "Reverend Choi, you are under arrest for the murders of Sangwoo Kang and Thomas DiGiorno. You have the right to remain silent."

CHAPTER 39 WHY PAY MORE?

"SO, WITH DECLINING offerings, why would they want to pay the national church more than they were required to?" Carter posed to Jason as they waited for their check at the Hungry Bear diner.

"Maybe they wanted to misrepresent the membership numbers to avoid discovery of Gethsemane's problems," Jason suggested. "If the membership numbers kept dropping it could have led to Choi's removal."

"Why would that have been a problem? With the church in chaos, wouldn't replacing Choi be better for all concerned? Why would Kwon, the most senior elder, go so out on a limb? Was it loyalty or something else?"

"You think Kwon and Choi were co-conspirators in ripping off church funds?"

"If Choi was taking any significant money from the church he could not do it alone. He would need Kwon's help, at least."

"I'll get this," Carter said when the check arrived. Jason dropped the tip. Carter grabbed his coat. "Let's go. I think we need to have a conversation with Elder Kwon."

CHAPTER 40 ELDER KWON

"MR. KWON, thank you for agreeing to meet with us here at Gethsemane today," Carter said, flanked by Jason in the Elder's office.

"It would be best if we conclude this distasteful matter as quickly as possible and let our church return to normal, Mr. Brand. A church is a business as well as a house of worship and operating without our financial documents has been most difficult. What more are you looking for?"

"We're hoping you can shed some light on a few questions Detective Kim and I have been wondering about. If you prefer, he can translate our conversation."

"That will not be necessary, Inspector. I'm sure you will keep your words simple enough," he said coolly.

Jason set down a cup of water on the desktop in front of the Elder. Carter paused for a moment to collect his thoughts before beginning the interview.

"Mr. Kwon, I'm sure you have learned by now that we have arrested *Moksanim* for the Lake Calhoun murders. We have questions regarding the church's finances that you are probably in the best position to answer."

Kwon took a sip of water. "What information are you looking for, Inspector? Mrs. Park informed me that she had a copy of the accountant's audit delivered to your office last week and your men confiscated the documents that were examined for that audit."

"Yes sir, all the figures looked in order but there are questions that the report did not address."

"Such as?"

"Such as why would you pay more money to the national church than your membership numbers would require?"

"We are an ethnic church, Inspector, and maintaining a good relationship with our American parent church is very important for us." Kwon was emphatic in his response.

"The audit showed your weekly offerings on a steady decline for months from about the time Dr. Kang began to make trouble," Jason said.

Kwon became silent and fixed his stare on Carter who stared at Kwon in return. "Yes, Mr. Brand, we were concerned that if the national church sensed trouble at Gethsemane they would replace Pastor Choi."

Elder Kwon's candidness took Carter by surprise. "Pastors are replaced all the time, Mr. Kwon. Why would you be so determined to prevent Reverend Choi's removal? From what I've heard, half the congregation would have welcomed a change in leadership."

"Would I be mistaken if thought that you suspect a conspiracy of some sort?"

"Let's just say that there are obvious questions that require reasonable answers," Carter replied.

Shame's Evidence

Elder Kwon reached into his desk drawer and took out a letter-size manila envelope. He carefully opened it and placed the contents on the desktop in front of Carter. "This was *Moksanim*'s son, Sung-Jin," Kwon said, holding up a 4 x 5 color photograph. "His mother, Choi *Samonim*, loved him very much. *Moksanim* loved him as well, but in a different way – much more strict. 'Tougher love' I believe is the expression. It was the opposite from most Korean families where it's the mother who puts the strong pressure on the children to make high scores in studies to get into the best colleges. Success in America was very important to Reverend Choi. When he was a young man he joined the Korean army and went into seminary because his test scores were not high enough for Seoul University or Yonsei University."

Carter was growing impatient. "Might I ask what bearing this has on the issue at hand?"

"Inspector, I referred to Sung-Jin in the past tense. He took his own life five years ago. *Samonim* died shortly after. The official cause of her death was cancer, but we who knew her sensed that the grief from her son's suicide was too much for her to bear."

"I'm very sorry to hear that, Mr. Kwon, but forgive me if I still don't see the relevance."

"Nor should you be expected to, Inspector. You see, Choi Sung-Jin came home from college for spring break and informed his parents that he was a homosexual. Before she passed away, *Samonim* told me that after her son's confession *Moksanim* flew into a rage and threatened to disown him; cut him off and throw him out of the house. She was much gentler. She hugged him and comforted him. *Moksanim* told me she had read chapter fifteen from the book of Luke to him, The Lost Son, and after that *Moksanim* broke down and cried. They all cried and hugged together."

"Mr. Kwon..." Carter interrupted. Kwon continued.

"Sung-Jin began attending services at Gethsemane with his partner, a Caucasian man. If there were members who objected to their presence, only Dr. Kang complained publicly. He constantly argued to the elders and deacons that Sung-Jin would be desecrating the sanctuary if he were allowed to enter and worship there. Kang would put leaflets on the windshields of cars in the parking lot during Sunday services with verses from scripture, in English and *hangul,* condemning Sung-Jin in the most hateful ways.

One day *Moksanim* received a call from the police at Sung-Jin's college. He had hung himself in his dormitory room closet. *Moksanim* never forgave Dr. Kang for his cruelty towards his son and blamed him for Sung-Jin's death."

"Honestly, Mr. Kwon, that information, if anything, only strengthens the case against Reverend Choi."

"Inspector, after the death of his son and his wife, *Moksanim* was a changed man. He knew that what first generation Korean-American parents were doing to their children was wrong. We, the first generation Korean-Americans, are so afraid that our children will not be who we want them to be that we deny them what we call their *kaesung*: their individuality.

Having a special identity is important to American people but quite foreign to our culture. My wife gave me two children but we are childless. They made me and my wife proud by graduating from Ivy League colleges and getting good jobs afterwards but they have no love for us...maybe just a little respect and gratitude. We rarely see them. Before she died, *Moksanim* and *Samonim* would regularly speak at the youth worship and encourage the children to follow their own *kaesung*. Dr. Kang would use this as evidence that Reverend Choi was interfering with proper Korean parenting and should be replaced. Inspector, for the sake of the children, the ones born in America or who have no memory of Korea, the so-called one-point-five and two-point-zero children, I could not let Gethsemane fall back to the old ways. I did all I could to protect *Moksanim*. Does that answer your questions?"

Carter looked at the photograph of Sun-Jin. "Yes, Mr. Kwon, it does, and it raises even more."

CHAPTER 41 WORK GOES ON

CARTER BRAND SAT alone at his desk. It was over. There was nothing left to do. It took less than an hour for the Grand Jury to return an indictment of murder in the first degree against Reverend Choi. At the arraignment, Choi's bail was set at $250,000 which was put up by Elder Kwon using his own house as collateral. He also retained Philip Kim, the same lawyer representing Jessica Ahn, to handle Choi's defense. Kim was a hustling lawyer, but also a good one, which gave Carter a certain measure of comfort that Reverend Choi would not be convicted easily.

For Carter, arresting pastor Choi was like arresting his own father. In truth, arresting his father for murder would probably have been less agonizing than arresting the man who had been his spiritual guide, religious mentor and teacher of how a healthy faith could bring meaning and fulfillment to one's otherwise empty life. He was there for him so many times when he questioned his own value as a husband and as a human being. Pastor Choi never judged him, but like Jesus, offered relatable parallels for him to consider his disconcertion in greater contexts, sealing each conversation with just the right passage from scripture.

"Great work, Brand," Captain Cohen said, toasting Carter's foam coffee cup with his own. "How about taking a week off? Get in some fishing, you deserve it."

Carter stretched. "Thanks, Izzy. I could use the time off. I need to get away and let my head settle down. Maybe next week. I need to cleanup the Kang case paperwork."

"Let what's his name, Kim, do it. The Walleye are running in Tonka, Brand," Cohen said while walking away.

Maybe the Captain was right. The case had taken an emotional toll and he needed time and space to remind himself of who he was, if he ever really knew. He hadn't spoken to Hannah since she left a month ago. His church was in chaos, and Jeannie Park-Reed, who had become such a brace for his spirits was now more a person of interest in Kang's murder than the object of his affection.

To any objective party, the murder case against Reverend Choi was rock solid: he had motive, opportunity, and most damning, the murder weapon. So, why was he so convinced of Choi's innocence? Was it because of the pastor's insistence of his innocence despite the overwhelming evidence to the contrary and he knew the man to be honest and forthright, his sexual assignations notwithstanding?

Carter walked down the hallway to the conference room that had been the de facto command center for the Kang case. Jason was sorting the stacks of papers for refiling.

"What should we do with Kang's medical records?" Jason asked. "We didn't need to go through them after Choi's arrest."

"Yeah, let's just box it all up and send it back to the Sherriff's office. We can let Judge Prentiss decide what to do with it."

"Roger that," Jason said, and continued organizing the papers.

Carter thumbed through the stack of medical record folders checking the first names of the numerous tabs labeled "Kim" stopping at the folder marked KIM, SOO-JI. As much as he wanted to open it, there was no longer any justifiable need - at least not for him. And without legitimate cause, examining the records would violate HIPAA regulations as well as his agreement with Judge Prentiss.

There was a way: the Ahn-Benezek case.

"Jason, take Kang's records to my office. I'm going to Sixth Street to see ADA Campion."

CHAPTER 42 THE FACE

IT WAS AFTER eight and dark by the time Carter returned to his office from visiting Assistant District Attorney Campion for permission to open Dr. Kang's file on Soo-Ji Kim. She wasn't sure why he needed to see it since it appeared to be irrelevant to the murder case. And since Donald Benezek and Jessica Ahn had copped pleas for drug sale and possession, she was not inclined to support a search for the mysterious "Suzy". But, despite her misgivings, she had approved the request only out of deference to Carter's rank and tenure.

He opened the manila folder and examined the first page of basic patient data.

1. Name: Kim, Soo-Ji

2. Address: Sherman Way, North Hollywood, CA

3. Age: 22

4. Height: 5'7"

5. Weight: 125 lbs.

6. Procedure(s): Rhinoplasty, lower blepharoplasty, genioplasty, mammaplasty.

The second page contained Kang's surgical notes for each of the procedures. Taped to the upper left corner of the third page was a faded color snapshot of Soo-Ji Kim captioned "Before", looking very much like the picture Superintendent Lee held up to the camera during the video conference with Seoul. To the right was an area marked "After" with just the rough paper surface exposed indicating that the picture that once had been taped there had been subsequently ripped away.

Carter took a print from the video frame containing the picture of young Soo-Ji Kim out of his desk drawer and held it up against the snapshot in the medical record. It was clearly the same person.

Jason walked into Carter's office knocking perfunctorily on the door as he entered.

"What are you doing here?" a startled Carter asked.

"Winnie's at Daisy Scouts with Rebecca so I thought I'd come by the shop to keep an eye on you."

"Take a look at this. Campion gave me twenty-four hours to go through Kang's records. I think I found our Suzy."

Jason looked closely at the "Before" picture from the Soo-Ji Kim folder and the black and white print from the video conference. He studied each picture closely. "It's the same person."

"And look at the address on Kang's letterhead. He had an office on Wilshire Boulevard, in L.A. That's where he must have hooked up with Suzy."

"Where's the 'After' shot?"

"It's missing. We have less than twenty-four hours to have this record reviewed by a plastic surgeon. I want to know what was done to her face and how she might look today. Let's keep this just between us."

CHAPTER 43 MAKING SUZY

ELEVEN O'CLOCK the next morning, Carter arrived at the office of Dr. Samuel Perlman with the Soo-Ji Kim folder, five enlarged copies of her "Before" picture and a copy of her medical record with the name blacked out.

"Thank you for seeing me on such short notice, Doctor," Carter said. "Here is the medical record I spoke of on the telephone this morning."

Dr. Perlman adjusted his glasses and quickly perused the document. When he finished, he raised his glasses over his head. "Has this patient given permission for her record to be released to another physician?"

"She is a suspect in a number of cases. Under such circumstances we have the authority to examine her medical records without her consent. The fact is we don't even know where she is."

"And we've discussed the issue with both the District Attorney's office and a Hennepin County judge," Jason added.

The doctor looked at both of them skeptically then lowered his glasses. "Blepharoplasty, rhinoplasty, genioplasty, mammaplasty – my, your girl's had quite a bit of work."

"Can you make a rough sketch of what this patient might look like after these procedures?" Carter asked.

Pushing the folder towards Carter's side of the desk, the doctor exhaled. "That's a tall order, my friend. With new eyes, nose, chin and breasts, you would have an equal chance of sketching what she might look like now yourself. May I ask who her surgeon was?"

"This was Doctor Kang's patient. We think this girl might have been involved with his death."

"Well, that helps a bit, but just a little bit. He came from L.A. and cut with a classic Beverly Hills style - at least he tried to."

"Anything you can come up with would be appreciated," Carter said, and rose to shake Doctor Perlman's hand.

"Give me a few days. I'll see what I can do."

CHAPTER 44 SKETCHES

EIGHT O'CLOCK in the morning, two days later, Carter was back at Dr. Perlman's office. The doctor handed him a manila folder.

"I have five pictures for you, Inspector. The four in this folder are computer simulations from the photograph of the girl using different surgical parameters."

Carter laid the colorized 8 x 10 pictures on the desk and studied each one closely. "Doctor, these pictures are amazing. Each one looks like a completely different person."

"You are correct, Inspector. The person you are looking for could look like anyone right now." The doctor tossed a sketchbook across the desk. "While waiting for my wife I brushed some rust off my drawing skills and made you this sketch freehand."

Carter flipped open the cover and immediately felt his scalp crawl. It couldn't be, but how could it be anybody but her. Besotted by desire he had resisted connecting the crystal-clear points that formed the unmistakable outline of Jeannie Park-Reed. With the veil of insanity lifted it all made sense; every detail fell perfectly into place except one: why?

Without saying a word, Carter shook the doctor's hand and quickly left the office with the rolled-up sketch in his pocket.

Sweat saturated his shirt on that chilly, overcast day. He cruised the Prius back to the precinct drifting through Windom, Page, Hale, and Powder Horn. The doctor said the girl could look like anybody today. What were the odds that he had made such an accurate freehand portrait of Jeannie Park-Reed without ever seeing her? Did it really look that much like her or was it just a chimera conjured in his bedeviled mind.

He drove to Lake Calhoun and parked by the path leading to the wooded area where Kang's body was found. He ran to the spot, the veins in his head throbbing. He looked down. He looked out across Lake Calhoun. He ran back to the Prius and doubled back through Lynnhurst, Armitage, Bloomfield and finally to 153 Fisher where he sat with the motor running playing back in his mind every conversation, every document, every meeting since he walked into the Gethsemane Church sanctuary that Sunday morning.

Jeannie Park-Reed was Suzy Kim, and Soo-Ji Hong. Where did she come from? Why was she here? What did she want? He threw the Prius into gear and sped back to the precinct.

CHAPTER 45 ENHANCED VIDEO

CARTER SLID the tape of the video conference with Seoul police Superintendent Lee into the recorder and let it play from the beginning. He needed to be reminded about who Soo-Ji Kim was before she started life as Mrs. Jeffrey Reed. As the tape played, listening with the objective ears of a detective, Carter began to understand her as well as he knew Jeannie Park-Reed - maybe better.

He sat across from Jason at the table in conference room 'B', file folders, documents and the MacBook laptop computer between them.

"I got your email message," Jason said. "I had some enhancement done to the video we found on the memory stick. Here is a sequence of the few frames where the woman's face is at all visible. I enlarged them, adjusted the brightness and sharpness."

Carter clicked the mouse to advance to the next frame and held Dr. Perlman's sketch next to the monitor side-by-side with the video frame.

"Who's that?" Jason asked.

"Dr. Perlman's estimation of what Soo-Ji Kim might look like after her cosmetic surgery."

Jason opened his eyes wide. "And you think that's your ladyfriend, Jeannie Park-Reed, correct?"

"Let's go on the assumption that it is. Where does that leave us?"

"Where has Soo-Ji or Suzy's name come up?" Jason asked.

"Whoa, even if we're sure that Jeanie Park-Reed is actually this Soo-Ji Kim does it necessarily follow that it is the same Suzy we're looking for?"

Jason opened each case folder and quickly reviewed the documents, one-by-one. "Her name was found on Kang's cell phone, Kang was writing heartsick love letters to her, she was probably the one who called Jessica for drugs."

"Detective, that's quite a leap from love letters to murder. There is no hard evidence that the Suzy we're looking for - the one in Kang's SUV - is the Soo-Ji we're sure we have here. We're just assuming that Soo-Ji and Suzy are the same."

"But boss, Kang refers to her as Suzy in his letter. It all might be freakishly coincidental but don't you think it's most probable? Forgive my impudence, but I think you're stuck in denial."

Carter dug in his heels. "There is no motive!" Why would Jeannie Park-Reed, a brilliant, educated, deeply religious woman, commit murder? It just doesn't make sense."

"She's killed before. Remember the john in Bundang?"

"Lee said it was never corroborated. That hooker might have been just trying to save her own skin and offered up Soo-Ji."

"Fair enough, but, if you're right about her being in the video banging Choi, couldn't that provide the alibi he needs?" Jason asked.

"It could. I'll visit him after I confront Mrs. Park-Reed. In the meantime see what you can dig up on her and Jeff Reed's past: marriage license, school records, and immigration documents. She says she went to Vassar so give a call to their alumni department."

"Will do," Jason said.

CHAPTER 46 OF INTEREST

JEANNIE PARK-REED answered the phone on the first ring. "I have to see you today," Carter said softly, but deliberately. "We found new information and I'm not sure how, or even if, it relates to the case. Can I see you today?"

"Today is going to be rough, Carter. The church is completely upside down after Pastor Choi's arrest. The national church is sending a replacement next week so I'm swamped with things to prepare."

Carter persisted. "I wouldn't ask you if it was not very important, Jeannie."

"I'm very sorry, Carter, but today is out of the question," she said without a trace of warmth or affection.

"Then I have to insist, Mrs. Reed."

Seconds passed before she spoke. "Carter, what is this all about?" Her voice sounded weak, and maybe she intended it to.

"I really can't discuss it over the phone, Jeannie. Would you prefer I come to see you or should I send someone for you?"

"Are you arresting me Carter?" she asked, her voice trembling. "Am I a suspect now?"

Her distress pulled hard on his gut. "No, Jeannie, we just have to talk."

"About what, Carter?" Jeannie pleaded.

"I'll see you at your office, Jeannie - four o'clock." Carter hung up the phone.

Jeannie was on the phone when Carter arrived at her church office at 4:10. She acknowledged his presence with a gesture for him to take a seat and wait for her to finish. From a chair in front of her desk he found an empty USB port on the back of her desktop PC where he could insert the memory stick containing the video.

Jeannie drummed the eraser end of her pencil on the desk blotter. Carter bounced his crossed leg, checking his watch every five minutes. Jeannie continued her phone conversation, speaking in Korean sprinkled with too few English nouns to indicate to whom she might be speaking, what about, or when the conversation might end.

She ended the call and as she parked the handset in the cradle she looked up at Carter, her eyes morphing from blank to worry to cheerful. Carter's fixed expression was all business.

"I have something to show you, Jeannie. I'm hoping you can shed some light on what we're looking at. May I use your computer?"

Jennie balked. "I have lots of important files here, Carter, what are we going to look at? Do you have a disk?"

"No, just a memory stick. I can plug it in here?" he asked, as he brought it near the computer's port.

"Wait! I'm not sure that's such a good idea. Shouldn't we let the computer guys handle it?" Jeannie begged, her voice now panicked.

Carter continued, clumsily inserting the memory stick into the rectangular USB socket, inverting it several times before arriving at the correct orientation. *Bing-bong* confirmed it was properly in place and ready to reveal its contents. He reached over the desk to take control of the mouse.

Jeannie sat back in her seat staring at the monitor, nervously nibbling on her thumbnail.

Carter double-clicked the video file icon. The Windows Media Player launched. The video started. He sat on the front right corner of the desk, his attention alternating between the video and Jeannie, her gaze glued to the business card-sized movie but showing nothing to indicate any recognition of the action displayed. Back at the station, Jason had modified the video file to loop continuously, digitally zooming in on different parts of the scene at each iteration.

Jeannie raised a single eyebrow. "You came here to show me low-grade porn, Carter?"

Carter set his jaw. "We're looking at Reverend Choi's house, aren't we Jeannie?"

She said nothing; just stared straight into his eyes with a paralyzing look of contempt and betrayal. "It's quite dark," she blinked. "It might be."

Carter brought his thumb and forefinger to his weary eyelids and sighed. "The woman in the video, Jeannie, that's you, isn't it?"

In every competition there comes a point where a badly losing player realizes the only chance for victory is through an extreme change of strategy and tactics. Jeannie had reached that point. Her bottom lip quivered over her clenched jaw as tears slowly welled in the corners of her eyes.

Her head dropped to the berth of her crossed arms. Her well-practiced sobs were volleys of emotion released at intervals timed to maximize their effect.

Carter's face was fire. "What the hell is this all about, Jeannie?" She kept her face buried in her arms, her weeping now continuous. "How could you keep this from me? Does Jeff know? Was this a regular thing or was Kang just lucky to shoot this video on your special day?"

Jeannie struggled to regain enough composure to speak. "Carter, you have no idea what I've been through."

"What, Jeannie, what? Your husband couldn't do it for you anymore so you went for your *moksanim*? What, Jeannie? Please tell me!"

Through her tears, Jeannie's face hardened to a contemptuous glare. "You think you've got it all figured out, don't you, Inspector? The aging, neglected, sex-starved church *ajuma* sets her sights on the bereft pastor to satisfy her raging desires, is that how you see it? Open and shut case, right?"

"Jeannie," Carter said calmly, "we have become close, maybe closer than we had any right to, but dammit, how could you? I really want to understand. Please explain."

Jeannie slammed her hands on the desk. "Fine! You want the truth? Here it is. About six months ago I went to visit Pastor Choi. He had been very depressed for a number of weeks and everyone at Gethsemane was noticing it. His sermons had become shorter and totally lacked any inspirational content. It was a year to the day after his wife died of cancer and I didn't want him to be alone so I brought over some dinner - some leftover *kalbi chim* and homemade kimchi. He thanked me and asked me to stay and share the food with him. I declined, politely, and told him I needed to get back home to prepare dinner for Jeff. *Moksanim* had been drinking and when I turned to leave he pulled me to the floor. He raped me, Carter," Jeannie choked.

If it was true he needed to hold her and comfort her and tell her he understood her pain. But he could not believe her. "Jeannie, I want to give you the benefit of the doubt, to consider what I saw in any context that might make sense, but you did not appear to be acting under duress in the video. On the contrary, you looked to me like a very willing participant."

"I was ashamed and I did feel pity for him. He loved his wife so much and now he was all alone, his son gone. You were right about one thing, though. *Moksanim* did make me feel like a woman again, a desirable woman...like the ways you make me feel."

"Did he really rape you, Jeannie?"

Now fully composed, Jeannie paused. "Honestly, perhaps I could have resisted more, but I did not. Why did I not? Maybe some day it will dawn on me. Did I feel sorry for him or sorry for myself? Who's to know for sure and does it really matter?"

"Yes, it really does matter. Don't you think that I would want to know what else you are capable of doing if you didn't have a problem having sex with a grieving pastor old enough to be your father while you were still married to another pastor? Who the hell are you, Jeannie?"

"I'm a flawed child of God, Carter Brand, just as you are. You love me, don't you? I'm married to a Christian minister and you are a Christian man still married to a devout Christian woman yet you still want me, don't you."

Carter just stared down at his shoes and said nothing. She was right, of course. She probably knew from the moment she first saw him in church without Hannah that they would end up in this situation. She did not know how or when, but he knew that she knew it was inevitable.

"Yes," said Carter. "God forgive me."

Jeannie lifted Carter's chin. "He will need to forgive me as well."

"Jeannie, you know I must question Reverend Choi about this, don't you?"

She grasped Carter's arm. "Is that really necessary? What purpose would that serve?"

Carter removed her hand. He could no longer confide in her and, in fact, he should never have. "I'm afraid so, Jeannie." And that was all he said.

CHAPTER 47 JEFF

JEFF REED WAS in bed when Jeannie burst open his bedroom door. A young man was zipping up his trousers; an amyl nitrate inhaler lay carelessly unhidden on the night table.

"Are you completely out of your mind?" Jeannie screamed. The boy scurried away carrying his shoes.

"Brand is getting closer. He doesn't yet realize what he's close to but the last thing we need is for you to get caught fucking some kid right now! He has Kang's blackmail video. Didn't you erase his cell phone?"

"He's a Catholic boy and he's over eighteen. It's my business. You have your indulgences and I have mine. And yes, I made sure there was nothing on his phone after I shot him," Jeff said, nonchalantly, and brought a paper cup of wine to his lips.

Jeannie slapped the cup out of his hand. She grabbed his throat. "Look, you pathetic, sniveling queer, I've been planning this project for over a year and we're almost there, ALMOST THERE! After this I'm free - we're free - and I'm not going to let you fuck it up for me!" She ejected him to the bed. His head drooped.

"Sorry," he whimpered.

Jeannie pulled an index card from her bag. "Now listen to me. Next Saturday night you will login to the Northern Trust web site and schedule a SWIFT transfer to Altajir Bank to CreditSuisse from this account for five million dollars. Use the credentials on this card and don't make any mistakes or the account will be disabled. At ten o'clock be at American Airlines departure terminal three for our flight to Costa Rica. If you're not there at ten I'm leaving without you, am I clear?"

CHAPTER 48 RECOGNIZANCE

REVEREND CHOI PEERED under the security chain keeping his front door open a thin crack. He greeted Carter disconsolately. "Yes, may I help you?"

"*Moksanim*, it is very good to see you. May I come in and speak with you for a few minutes? "

He thought for a moment before responding. "Inspector, it would be most unwise to speak with you without my attorney present, would you not agree?"

"Yes, I would agree with you that by talking to the police right now you would be taking a risk, but I am here today more as a friend than a cop."

Choi studied Carter carefully and then unfastened the chain. "Please come in, Inspector." He led Carter to a dining room chair, motioned for him to sit then took a seat across the table from him. Incarceration and shame had not diminished his civility. "May I bring you something to drink? Some tea?"

"*Moksanim*, the woman in the video I showed you in your office that afternoon was not a prostitute from an escort service. It was Jeannie Park-Reed, wasn't it?"

Choi stood up and out of his chair and waved his hand towards the door. "Maybe this was a bad idea after all. Please leave now."

As Choi moved to escort him to the door, Carter rose from his seat and put his hand on his pastor's shoulder. "*Moksanim*, please, I did not come here today to humiliate you. I'm here to help you." Choi removed Carter's hand and returned to his seat, continuing to eye the policeman warily. "I realize that you did not identify Mrs. Reed because you wanted to protect her. Would that be an accurate assessment?" Choi nodded slowly. "Is it also true that you were willing to risk prison rather than betraying her?" Choi closed his eyes and nodded again. "Reverend, your involvement with Mrs. Reed concerns us only so far as she can provide the alibi for your time. Can you now tell me when you were with her on Monday, the fifteenth?"

"She would arrive every Monday precisely at nine o'clock in the evening – after her husband left for his youth group. After that I would sleep through the night."

"Dr. Kang was killed around ten o'clock that night. We checked your phone records and found that a call was placed to your home at ten forty-five. Do you recall that?"

"Honestly, Inspector, it was probably answered by the machine. I'm sure I was sleeping by then. I had a message from Mr. Kwon that night, I believe."

"OK, let's assume that you were home that evening. We still don't have a solid alibi other than your word. I expect that Mrs. Reed would not corroborate your testimony..."

"No! She must not be asked to testify!"

"Reverend, we are talking about your life, the rest of which could be spent behind bars!"

"So be it. I have done all that the Lord has called me to do. Now I just live on the pleasure of my memories. I have no life."

"Alright, *Moksanim*, alright. I'll find a different approach, but please have faith. I'll find a different way."

"Carter, my faith is all that I have left."

CHAPTER 49 LAX

THE DEPARTMENT WOULD not pay for Carter's trip to Los Angeles. Captain Cohen reminded him of the Larson case and how he had spent a considerable amount of time and department money to unsuccessfully prove the innocence of a woman accused of murdering her sister.

As far as anyone was concerned, especially ADA Campion, Reverend Choi was the undisputable killer of Dr. Kang and his conviction would be quick and easy. The cost of this fishing trip would have to come out of Carter's pocket.

He flicked on the radio and GPS in the rented Prius and entered the address of the Olympic Police station near Los Angeles's Koreatown. In need of virtual companionship, he selected "Jane" as the voice the GPS would use to call out directions. He had no idea what a "SIG alert" was and was unable to modify his route even if he did know, and having delegated responsibility for his timely arrival to the electronic Sacajawea in the dashboard, he mindlessly headed towards the Harbor Freeway.

He had been to Los Angeles just one time before and that was to meet Hannah's sister after Hannah had accepted his marriage proposal. With no other family in the U.S., meeting her sister was like seeking her mother's blessing in abstentia.

One hour and two SIG alerts later, he pulled into the Vermont Street parking lot. Lieutenant Rick Donovan met him at the door and glanced at his watch, his expensively coiffed blond hair holding its ground against the warm Santa Ana wind.

"I was getting worried that I might have given you the wrong address or directions."

"No, the directions were probably fine if I had followed them instead of listening to GPS girl who apparently was as clueless about SIG alerts as I was."

The lieutenant led Carter to a second-floor conference room equipped with its own robotic cappuccino machine. "Latte?" he asked.

"No thanks, I'm fine."

"You sure? It really is good. It makes plain coffee too...I think."

Carter declined with a polite wave of his hand. Donovan took a seat at the conference table across from Carter and closed his eyes dreamily as he savored a sip of his latte, leaving a frothy mustache over his upper lip. He tongue-swished it clean before sliding a file folder across the table to Carter.

"Here is the information I found in the computer files in response to your email, Inspector. It was a routine massage parlor raid, pretty much like any other we did back then. The owners would be busted for running a brothel and their lawyers would plea it down to a fine. The business interruption would be a few days, at most. Usually, the girls were released shortly after their night court appearance, unless they were caught in *flagrante delicto*, in which case they'd be fined and maybe spend a night in jail.

We checked the picture you sent against mug shots in the system and found a match. The arrest record is in your file folder. When she was busted we verified her name was Soo-Ji Hong from her green card. Now here's the weird part. Since she was caught in the act, we arrested her for prostitution and her john for solicitation. But it turns out that they were married so we had to let them go. The records should have been expunged but they never followed up so we still have the details. His name was Jeffery Reed, a student at Hollywood Theological Seminary."

"Do you have the address where they lived?" Carter asked.

"Mrs. Reed was a student at UCLA. They lived in the married students housing. Want to hear some more? A few months before, Jeffery Reed was picked up in West Hollywood for solicitation of a male prostitute and charged with a misdemeanor. If he had been charged after the massage parlor raid it would have been a second offense – a felony in the state of California."

"Jesus, that must have been quite a scene at the station when you discovered they were husband and wife. Do you mind if I hold onto the folder?"

"Please, it's your copy. Sorry you had to come all the way out here for just a five-minute chat. It's always a pleasure to get law enforcement visitors from other states but we could have had this conversation by phone or email," Donovan said while shaking Carter's hand.

"Actually, Lieutenant, I needed some time to clear my head...and I had to take care of some personal business here in L.A."

"Glad we could help. Enjoy your stay in Los Angeles," Donovan said and dialed-up another latte.

Back in his rented Prius, Carter tapped the address of the Hollywood Theological Seminary into the GPS with a map of Los Angeles unfolded on the passenger seat should he need to override Jane in the event of another SIG alert. With the Blackberry, he found the school's web site and shot off a quick email to the contact address listed to notify them of his imminent visit.

Five minutes on the Hollywood Freeway and another two on Sunset Boulevard later, Carter pulled into the parking lot of the Hollywood Theological Seminary, an aging three-story art deco structure with a freshly painted façade being the only evidence of any significant building maintenance. An old man in stained, white, overalls kneeling between wings of the revolving door held up his hand for Carter to wait until he finished oiling the center shaft. After finishing, he motioned for Carter to push through and frowned as the door still screeched rudely in defiance of its fresh lubrication.

The round reception desk facing the revolving door was unmanned, requiring Carter to scan the directory for the location of Dr. Reggie Hudson, president of the seminary. His office was on the second floor. Carter rang for the elevator and waited. After a few minutes he pressed the call button rapidly three or four times in a futile attempt to jolt the ancient mechanism into operation. Hearing not a sound, he headed for the stairs and climbed the twenty steps, favoring his still-bruised hip.

Carter tapped on the office door near the top of the staircase. Dr. Hudson, a white-haired black man, snored at his desk having nodded out before he could press the enter key to send an email reply. A traditional hymn was playing on the radio through tinny plastic speakers. He put on his glasses and squinted at Carter, lowered the radio then waved for him to come in. Carter reached across the desk to shake his hand.

"Inspector Brand, welcome," Dr. Hudson said. "Please sit down. I would offer you some coffee but we seem to be out right now. Can I send out for some?"

"I'm fine, really," Carter replied, "but thank you just the same."

"I received your email and will do all I can to help you out. But you must understand that there are some areas involving former students that must remain confidential."

"Yes, I understand. I'll try to keep my questions confined to general information. What can you tell me about Jeffery Reed?"

Dr. Hudson turned to his computer screen and clicked through randomly organized folders until he found a file named "J. Reed". He straightened his glasses. "Let me see. Mr. Reed enrolled twelve years ago with an Associates degree in history from a community college in Minneapolis. Normally we don't accept students into the Masters of Divinity program with less than a B.A. degree, but it says here that he had significant experience as a lay teacher at a parish in Winona, Minnesota. He graduated two years later with an M.Div."

"Do you have dormitories here? Did he live on campus?"

"We really don't have much of a campus here, per se, Inspector. Most of our students live in town in rented apartments or houses."

"Would you be able to tell where he lived?"

"Hmm, yes, I have two addresses for him here. One is on Pico and the other is on the UCLA campus. Does that mean anything to you?"

"Yes, it does. Would you have any way of telling if he shared an apartment or house with anyone before he moved to the UCLA address?"

Hudson frowned. "While our files are held in the computer, the organization of them leaves quite a bit to be desired, I'm afraid. Can I get back to you with that information?"

A short, gray-haired woman of about seventy came into Hudson's office carrying two steaming mugs.

"I took the liberty of bringing some tea for you and your guest, Doctor," the woman said, and placed the cups on the desk. She turned to leave.

"Mrs. Wilson?" Hudson called out. "Thank you - that was very kind of you. Do you recall a student named Jeffery Reed? Studied here about ten years ago?"

The woman paused. "I think so. From the mid-west, I recall; a very sweet boy. He married a Korean student at the university, I believe."

"Yes," said Carter, "that would be correct. You wouldn't happen to recall who he roomed with before he married, would you?"

"Come to think of it, I do remember. It was Billy Mehan. He's now the pastor at Orange Community Church in West Hollywood. They were roommates and very good friends."

"The OCC church is on Fountain Avenue, not far from here," Hudson said.

Carter thanked him and rose to leave "Is it safe to assume that the elevator is out of order?"

"Luck of the draw," Dr. Hudson said with a shrug.

It was a pleasantly warm late afternoon. The Santa Ana wind was now just a breeze. Carter retrieved an L.A. street map from the car and headed off to the Orange Community Church on foot.

The walk was unsettling. Under an overcast sky the daylight denizens of Sunset Boulevard loitering outside boxy, grey buildings cast long shadows on the sidewalk murdering any suggestion of a palm tree-lined paradise. This was hell's incubator where real lives struggled to achieve and keep harmony with a dubious culture. This was where ten years ago the story lines of Soo-Ji Kim, Jeffery Reed and Sangwoo Kang converged.

Carter's hip was beginning to cramp as he arrived at the church. He had not called ahead for an appointment. Two women holding hands on the front steps directed him to the sanctuary where he might find Pastor Mehan. He found the man standing behind a simple oak pulpit dressed in nicely-pressed vestments, a multi-colored crocheted stole over his shoulders, studying papers that Carter assumed was a new or previously preached sermon. His blond hair was closely cropped and his beard and mustache well-groomed.

The pastor looked up and greeted Carter. "Welcome to Orange Church, friend. May I help you with something?"

"I'm here from Minneapolis, Reverend. I apologize for not phoning in advance but this visit was not planned. I've just met with Dr. Hudson at the Hollywood Seminary and he thought it would be valuable if we spoke. Is there somewhere we can talk privately?"

"Of course, Mr..."

"Brand, Carter Brand. I am an Inspector with the Minneapolis police department here investigating a homicide back home."

The pastor stepped down from the pulpit and led Carter to a cramped office just outside the sanctuary entrance. Carter took a seat in front of a chipped mahogany desk cluttered with news clippings, magazines and hand written notes.

"Might I assume you are here regarding a matter involving Jeffery Reed, Inspector?"

"Yes, that would be correct, Reverend. Would you mind answering a few questions?"

"If I can. I'm sure you understand that confidentiality and discretion will border our conversation."

"Reverend Mehan, I understand that you shared an apartment with Jeffery Reed when you both attended seminary. How well did you know him?"

"I knew him probably better than anyone. We were lovers, Mr. Brand. It was a very complex relationship. I was - am - a gay man. For Jeffery, being the son of a minister, it was far more difficult for him to admit to himself who he was than it was for me."

"I don't understand, Reverend. Jeffery Reed is a married man - married to a woman. Are you saying he is bisexual?"

Mehan answered haltingly. "He is sexual...but never with me...we were intimate...but he never...he always stopped short of sexual intercourse. I think he believed it was a hedge against eternal damnation to be sexually free in all respects except for the explicit sex act. It was a line he would never cross. He had to leave his home town in Minnesota because of rumors that he was having an affair with a teenage boy. His father, the pastor at the church where Jeffery taught Sunday school, basically threw him out of the house and pulled strings to get him into the Hollywood Seminary. He hoped it would straighten his son out, you know, intense Christian tough love."

"So, how did he hook up with Suzy Kim?"

"He was determined to be a straight male with normal male urges. More than anything, he wanted to live a conventional life and not displease his family. He would visit houses of prostitution frequently hoping to find a girl who could arouse him sexually but he never found one. One day he came back very excited from a visit to a massage parlor in Koreatown. He said he met the most amazing girl who made him feel like a real man was supposed to feel and maybe he was finally cured. A few months later they were married and he was gone. We graduated soon after that and he sent me a letter to tell me that he had found a position as an English Ministry pastor in a Korean church in Colorado Springs."

"Did he mention the name of the church?"

"Yes, Inspector, but that information I will have to keep confidential."

"Thank you, Reverend. This has been a very valuable conversation," Carter said, reaching over the desk to shake Pastor Mehan's hand before leaving.

"I'm glad I could help, inspector. If you see Jeffery would you send him my very best wishes and that he is always in my prayers?"

Carter nodded. "Yes, Reverend, you can count on that."

CHAPTER 50 AU PAIR

THE U.C.L.A. DEAN of Students needed to escalate the request all the way up to the Provost's office before she would accede with Carter's request to see the college file on Susan Kim and then only after a call from Lieutenant Donovan verifying his identity and purpose. Prohibited from removing or copying the file documents, Carter examined them in a conference room, snapping pictures and jotting notes into his Blackberry.

Susan Kim had applied when she was seventeen years old with perfect S.A.T. scores and a transcript with honor role grades and glowing recommendations from teachers at Burbank High School. Her home address was on Buena Vista Boulevard, in Burbank. She graduated from U.C.L.A. magna cum laude four years later with a bachelor's degree in international finance.

Her parents were listed as "Deceased" but the local contact name she gave was a Nora Teitlebaum living at the same Buena Vista Boulevard address. With his Blackberry, he checked through the Internet to see if the Teitlebaums still lived there. They did.

An hour later, Carter pulled into the Teitlebaum's driveway after a thankfully uncomplicated GPS-guided trip from the U.C.L.A. campus. Nora Teitlebaum, forty-ish and flirting with obesity, with graying hair peeking from under her crocheted head covering, welcomed him in.

"What a marvelous surprise!" she said, shaking Carter's hand warmly with both of hers. "We had not heard anything from our Susan in over ten years. Have you seen her? You said you were from Minneapolis. Is that where she is living now? Is she well?"

"Yes, she is well," Carter answered affirmatively to avoid unnecessarily upsetting his host. He accepted a seat on a plastic-upholstered sofa and proceeded delicately. "There was a homicide in Minneapolis, Mrs. Teitlebaum. I'm here in L.A. to investigate the backgrounds of people who might have had some involvement."

She gasped. "Is Susan in trouble?"

"Mrs. Teitlebaum, what was your relationship with Susan? How did she come to live here?"

"Inspector - Brand was it? - after Shoshanna left for college I wanted to go back to work to help out with the bills. Believe you me, four years at Vassar was going to be expensive, even with her scholarship money. A friend mentioned to me that she had used an au pair to help her out after her baby was born and maybe I could hire one to help me out, even though we had no young children to care for.

She referred me to an agency in Los Angeles that she had used a few years back. We were introduced to Susan who had recently arrived from Korea. She was really much younger than the person we were looking for at the time and we couldn't check her references because they were all from Korea. But she was so charming and enthusiastic that we decided to give her a try. We were concerned about her English fluency, of course, but that turned out not to be a problem. Her command of the English language wasn't bad and only improved over time. She even taught my kids some Korean words. Now they call me '*umma*.'"

"How long did she live here?"

"Until she graduated high school. She got a full scholarship to U.C.L.A. and moved to a dormitory on campus. I guess she was about eighteen then. No, wait, she was only seventeen. That's right, she finished high school a year early." Mrs. Teitlebaum reached over to an end table, opened a fat photo album and flipped through the pages until she located the photograph she was looking for. She showed Carter the picture of Suzy in a white graduation gown with a gold tassel on the cap posing on the high school steps with the Teitlebaum family. Even without directly comparing the picture with the one taken of Soo-Ji Kim before the surgery, the prominent bump on her nose confirmed identification.

A tear welled in Mrs. Teitlebaum's eye. "I'm sorry, Mr. Brand. We loved that little girl so much. She was like a daughter to me. The kids thought of her as their older sister. I don't know how I would have gotten along without her back then. She cooked, cleaned and did the shopping. And, oy, she was such a quick study. She learned to cook Jewish so well that everyone insisted she do the cooking on the high holy days instead of me - instead of me!" she laughed.

"I'm confused. If Susan took care of the kids and housework during the day when did she have time to attend high school?"

"She would go to school in the morning with my other three. They were old enough to take care of themselves until

Susan got home. After a while, Eli, my husband, had his classes switched to the evening. He taught accounting at the community college. That left him free to help Susan take care of the kids during the day. He would help her with her schoolwork until I got home from work. She really appreciated that. You could tell how grateful she was."

"Did you stay in touch after she left?"

"For a while. After she left for college she would call and write and visit often for a few years and then she just disappeared, poof, into thin air. We tried to find her but no one would give us any information. Please, inspector, if you see her, please send her our warmest wishes and tell her how much we miss her. Will you do that?"

Mrs. Teitlebaum's anguish penetrated Carter's emotional armor rendering him silent and contemplative. Something had happened to Suzy Kim in the years between Buena Vista Boulevard and U.C.L.A. that turned this bright and promising human being into a calculating, evil, predatory creature. Was it the baggage she brought with her that persisted despite the Teitlebaum's loving acceptance? Or was it something else?

"Mrs. Teitlebaum, where did Susan sleep when she was here? Did she have her own room?"

"Tch, of course. We moved the junk in the attic to the basement and made a cozy bedroom for her up there. It was a nice room - very sunny most days. She would read and do her homework up there. It was so quiet."

"You said your husband works at night. Do you think I might be able to speak with him today?"

She snickered. "Only if you're part Gypsy. Eli's been dead for over eight years."

"I'm very sorry to hear that, Mrs. Teitlebaum. Was he ill?"

"No, no, just a random act of violence the police said. In the wrong place at the wrong time or maybe the right place at the wrong time, I don't know. He was at home alone for lunch when they came into our house. I guess the burglars decided that our house looked appealing so they pushed the door in and stabbed Eli before they robbed us. They took all my jewelry and any cash we had around. The place was a mess after they went through all the drawers. I still don't know why they had to kill him. Eli would not have fought them, for God's sake. We have insurance."

"Susan was away at school?"

"Yes, Inspector. The last time we saw her was at Eli's funeral. You could tell how distraught she was...she could barely speak. They were very close, you see."

Carter rose to leave. "Thank you very much for your time, Mrs. Teitlebaum. I'm sorry to have brought back such painful memories."

"Oh, psh! I've gotten over losing Eli a long time ago. You brought happiness to me today with news about our Susan. If you should speak with her would you ask her if we could get in touch with her? You know, I have a Facebook page. Maybe she would allow me to Friend her? Would you ask her?"

"Yes, Mrs. Teitlebaum. I promise that."

Sitting in his car, Carter thought about the trail of blood that followed Suzy Kim, from that apartment in Seoul to Minneapolis: the drunken john in Bundang, Eli Teitlebaum, Dr. Kang, the hardwood floor salesman. How many more were there?

CHAPTER 51 LUCY

WHEN HE SAW Hannah off to Los Angeles a month ago, Carter never expected to soon be there himself. But there he was and somewhere in the San Fernando Valley was she. His feelings towards her were unchanged and had he not been in the eye of the JPR hurricane he would have made a point to see her during his time in Los Angeles. The fact of the matter was that he would have no idea what to say to her if, or when, they met.

He had to see her. If there was any chance of them ever reconciling it was imperative that he see her before leaving L.A. if only to exchange a quick hello and goodbye.

Hannah's sister, Lucy Lee, was a woman of singular dynamism. She had come to America fifteen years ago when she was only nineteen, married and divorced a scion of a sizeable California real estate empire parlaying the settlement into substantial investments in property and local Korean businesses. Through the employment agency she owned, she was able to secure for Hannah an H1B work visa and a job at a Minneapolis hospital despite the fact that her sister had only two years of formal nursing training in Korea. As modest and unassuming as Hannah was Lucy was shrewd and driven; a no-nonsense hustler and nobody's fool.

It was 2PM and his flight at LAX was at six. Carter rolled his Blackberry's cursor to the address book, scrolled to the Lucy Lee entry and thumbed down the track ball button to make the call. He let it ring exactly twenty times. Lucy did not believe in answering machines. If anyone really needed to get in touch with her they could call her cell phone, the number of which she rarely gave out and changed often. For close friends and family, though, she had a special arrangement where the caller would let the phone ring precisely twenty times, hang up, and then call back immediately. Following the protocol, he ended the call, waited exactly fifteen seconds, and then placed the call again. Lucy answered on the first ring.

"What do you want Carter?" Lucy said, coldly.

"I...I was just in town for a few hours and thought I'd give my wife a call."

"You just happened to be in town and thought you had *better* give your wife a call. Isn't that what you really meant to say?"

"I don't know, Lucy. Things are very confused right now. Maybe you're right, I just don't know."

"Yeah, well I know. What I don't know is why I convinced my parents to give their blessing to your marriage to my sister in the first place. They told me that Americans always get divorced but I promised them that you were different. Now I see that I was wrong. You're just a wimpy, worthless American man who doesn't know the meaning of the word commitment. Why did you marry her? Did you really love her or did you just want a free live-in nurse after she took care of you in the hospital when you were stabbed.

She loved you, Carter, which is why I argued to our parents on her behalf, not yours."

Carter turned defensive. "Lucy, that's a pretty strong accusation from a woman who traded in her husband for a fat bank account."

"Listen, Carter Brand, my sister is not me, do you understand? She is good and kind and deserves a better man than you!"

"I know that. You're probably right, but I still love her and she is still my wife. Can I stop by and see her today? I have just a few hours before my plane leaves."

"Well, well, isn't that just so white of you. You managed to spare a few hours to be with your wife that you haven't seen in a month. God forbid you should miss your plane. Drop dead, you creep."

"Lucy, I appreciate you taking care of Hannah while we work things out but this is a private matter between us and I would prefer to keep it that way."

"Well, she's not home right now. She's at the doctor's office."

Carter's heart quickened. "Doctor? Is she alright?"

"Why should you care?"

"Because she's my wife, dammit!"

"She's fine - just finding a woman's doctor in case she needs to stay here much longer. She's going to the mall after that so I don't expect her back til after six but I'll tell her you called, OK? Nice talking to you, Carter." She hung up the phone.

"Hello? Lucy? Lucy?" Carter repeated into the Blackberry until the DISCONNECTED text appeared on the display. He instinctively moved his thumb to the

REDIAL button but stopped before pressing it. Further conversation would serve no purpose.

CHAPTER 52 COLORADO SPRINGS

SITTING IN A Delta Airlines boarding gate in Denver, Carter clutched his Blackberry waiting for an update from Jason on Korean churches in Colorado Springs. The blinking red LED told him the message had arrived. He thumbed-down the trackball to read it:

> *Boss, I spoke with a woman who answered the phone at the Second Korean Presbyterian Church, on Monterey Drive. She confirmed that a Jeffery Reed had been employed there a number of years ago. While on hold I heard some muffled conversation in Korean that I could not make out. After that she came back and said she was mistaken about Jeffery Reed working there. The Pastor's name is Hyun. Maybe you should pay him a visit?*
>
> *Kim*

Forty minutes later, Carter loosened his seat belt in economy class seat 17-C, on the aisle, as the Boeing 737 leveled off at cruising altitude. Sitting next him in seat 17-B was a twenty-ish young woman who appeared to be in her late months of pregnancy. Next to her in 17-A was her five year-old son tossing in the air a small, spongy football marked with a green cross and the words "Steadfast & Loyal".

Carter opened a two month-old copy of *The Atlantic Monthly* magazine. The little boy's football plopped onto the crease. With rage-corked eyes the mother slapped the little boy across the face with the full force of the back of her hand. He wailed. She cocked her hand again and held it threateningly above his head.

"You want more?" The boy strained to control his tears. "Here, Cody," she said, and dropped a half-eaten Hershey bar onto the little boy's lap.

She turned to a horrified Carter who sat speechless. "I'm sorry, sir," she said with a distinct Southern twang. "That boy makes me crazy sometimes."

Carter closed his magazine. "Excuse me, young lady. I have no children, and am probably in no position to offer advice, but don't you think that reaction was severe?"

Her polite smile disappeared as she sized-up Carter while considering an appropriate response. "Sir, we are Christian people and raise our children as scripture tells us. We don't have any need for big-headed advice from city liberals who train their kids to be spoiled, sinful and weak. And you *are* right. If you never had kids you wouldn't know about any of this."

Carter wanted to just let the matter end there and return to the magazine article he had just begun to read, but glancing over at the chocolate-smeared face of the little boy, he felt compelled to respond.

"I consider myself a good Christian man and while I don't profess to be a biblical scholar, I'm pretty certain that the Holy Book does not command parents to beat their children in public like that."

She answered directly. "Sir, if you had read the book of Proverbs you would know: *He who spares the rod hates his son and he who loves him is careful to discipline him.*" She pulled a large Bible out of her bag and quickly flipped through the dog-eared and bookmarked pages running her index finger over the text searching for an appropriate passage. "And, *If you punish him with the rod, he will not die.*" Her voice grew louder with each verse. Then she paused and looked down at her lap before reciting a final passage. She began to sob. "*Punish him with the rod...and save his soul from death...* I'm sorry, sir."

Carter asked a flight attendant for a tissue and handed it to the girl. She wiped her eyes and blew here nose.

"My husband, Specialist First Class Richard Mendoza, is at Fort Carson. He's being sent to Iraq tomorrow. The baby is due next month. If something happens to him what will I do, what can I do?"

Carter had no answer - not even a disposable word of assurance. While most people considered him a "really nice guy", the ability to give them emotional comfort when they needed it most was a quality that Carter knew he was sorely lacking. He handed her another tissue.

"Thanks," she said. "I guess I just need to trust in the Lord, right?"

"What else can we do?" Carter confirmed.

The plane pitched up then dropped suddenly and continued bouncing through the turbulent air, wings flapping, drinks flying. The pilot lit the seatbelt sign and spoke on the P.A. to calm the passengers. "Folks, we've got a good chop for the next five minutes, or so, as we fly over the mountains.

Please stay in your seat with your seatbelt securely fastened. We'll see if we can get clearance for a more favorable altitude."

The terrified young woman was now absorbed in intense prayer with her eyes tightly closed. Cody slept. The plane descended and the turbulence calmed as the woman said "amen." Carter took the young woman's hand and smiled. She smiled back.

The frigid, dry Colorado Springs air stung Carter's cheeks as he stood on the taxi line outside the terminal building. Cold and impatient, he walked down the line to the first car available.

The driver rolled down his window unleashing a blast of hot, foul air that enveloped Carter's face.

"You wanna put that bag in the trunk?"

"That's OK, it's small. I'll hold onto it."

"Suit yourself. Where to?"

Carter scanned the Blackberry's inbox for Jason's message with the address of the Second Korean Presbyterian Church and read it to the driver.

"Monterey, that's near Ventura, right?" the driver asked.

"Beats me. I'm not from around here."

The driver keyed the address into the windshield-mounted GPS unit. Considering the rundown condition and smell of the vehicle, Carter guessed the navigational device was more of a necessity than a luxury. The cab reeked of the funkiest compound of odors the components of which became distinct with each waft of the stale, hyper-heated air: cigarettes, B.O., fast food and marijuana. Clearly, this 30-ish, long-wavy-haired driver spent a large portion of his waking hours, and probably a good many non-waking hours, in the comfort of his mobile money-maker. Carter lowered the window just enough to vent the stench without overtly giving offense to the driver. "Here for the Evangelical Conference?" the driver asked.

"No, what conference?"

"Dr. Wahnsig's Christ Congress. Popular a few years back but the attendance has gone downhill since the scandals. It was great for the cabbies. Cleaned up back then."

"Is that the same Wahnsig who wrote a book on child psychology?"

"Yeah, a manual on how to whip your kids. The book every parent followed here for awhile. Problem was, it started to be easier for parents to just haul off and smack their kids instead of showing them love or patience or attention. Seems like for the tough love crowd showing toughness is easier than showing love. Got any kids?"

"No, not yet."

"Not yet? No offense dude, but the clock's running. What are you, about fifty?"

"About."

"Well, it's none of my business but if you still plan to have kids you better get on the hump – no pun intended. Married?"

"Yes. What about you? Married? Kids?" Carter asked, hoping to reverse the direction of conversation.

"No and yes. My little boy lives with his mom. She lives with this fundamentalist wacko who used to spank my son, Maxwell, every chance he got; thought it would teach him respect for authority. Max is a good kid, a really smart one, too, and never a discipline problem 'til they moved in with this asshole. I went to pick him up one weekend and he had this big, red welt on the side of his face. I jacked that mayonnaise motherfucker up against the wall and told him I'd beat the shit out of him if he ever touched my kid again."

"Did he?"

"No, just prays for him – and me, I'm told."

Carter checked his watch. "So, how did you end up in the cab business?"

"I got a job offer out here for a defense contractor after I defended my dissertation at the University of Chicago."

Carter raised his eyebrows. "Dissertation?"

"Yeah, spent enough time in school. Figured it was time to stop pissing away my folk's money and start earning."

"What's your degree in?"

"PhD in math, statistics, believe it or not."

"Hey, why not. What happened to your defense job?"

"Quit. I was given an assignment to determine which weapons would produce the highest probability of casualties. Not deaths, mind you, injuries. A very devout Christian manager - another wacko - explained that killing an enemy only puts two of his comrades out of the action, on average. But if you just wound him, it takes five people, or more, to care for him and remove him from battle. So, it is militarily more advantageous to just grievously wound your enemy than to kill him outright."

"Is that right? That's pretty cold blooded."

"Yeah. They would bring a local pastor in once a week to allow all the weapons developers to get in touch with their feelings of guilt."

"How did they reconcile that work with their Christian faith?"

"Who knows. You can read into scripture whatever happens to serve your purpose. So, what do you do, man?"

"I'm a cop in Minnesota."

"Really? You don't look much like a beat pounder. Detective?"

"Yeah, Inspector."

"I guess you're kind of in the probability business yourself, right? You can probably tell from experience the type of person who most likely committed the crime, right?"

"That's called profiling. Can't do that."

"But you do it anyway, right?"

"Usually, but sometimes it turns out to be not at all who you expect."

The taxi pulled up to the church. "Is this the place? It's a Korean church, ya know."

"Yes, I hear the pastor gives one hell of a sermon." He handed the driver a five-dollar tip on top of the fare. The driver accepted the generous gratuity and gave Carter a stained and wrinkled business card.

"Hey, thanks, man. When you need to leave here give me a call. My cell number's written on the back."

Carter walked around the grounds for a few minutes to vent his smellish clothing before entering the church. Pastor Hyun was greeting the last of the Korean worshippers exiting the sanctuary as Carter walked through the church's front door. "Welcome to our church, friend," the Pastor said. "The Korean service has just finished but I assume you are hear for the EM service, yes? It is down the hall on the right."

"Thank you, Reverend. Yes, I'm looking for the English Ministry service."

The pastor gave Carter a quick look of scrutiny, sweeping him from his head to his shoes. "I haven't seen you here before. Is this your first time?"

"Actually, I'm just in town for a short while and thought I'd lookup and old friend who I remember attends church here."

"Really? What brings you to Colorado Springs?"

Carter fumbled. "Um, I'm here for...the Christian Congress. I'll be leaving after that."

"Well, maybe I will see you there," he said, shaking Carter's hand. "Who is your friend? If I see him I will tell him you were here."

"Friend? Yes, that would be Kim, Mr. Kim."

"We have quite a few members with the name Kim, Mr....?"

"Brand, Carter Brand. His first name is Clarence, Clarence Kim."

"Are you sure, Mr. Brand? I don't think I've heard of a Korean man named Kim here with a first name Clarence."

"Yes, you're right, Reverend. We were friends in college and he wanted an American name to fit in with our crowd. He played saxophone so he took the name of his favorite sax player," Carter said, hoping the explanation would be outrageous enough to halt any further conversation. It was.

Hyun shrugged, "Well, Carter Brand, I hope you find him and you find the Congress spiritually fulfilling. Enjoy your stay."

Carter walked down the hallway to the English Ministry sanctuary and accepted a copy of the service bulletin from an usher at the entrance. He found a seat in the back row. On stage a young man of about nineteen with a badly pockmarked face was feverishly strumming a popular Christian song on an acoustic guitar. To his right stood a heavy young man, about the same age, with thick glasses, plucking an electric bass. Behind them, a pale girl in her early twenties carried the melody on an electric piano.

"God is good?" the acoustic guitar player quizzed the membership.

"All the time!" came the corporate response, prompting Pastor Warren Goode to begin his sermon.

"Thanks be to the Lord for our outstanding praise band, amen?" the pastor said at the podium, applauding as the musicians left the stage. He adjusted his glasses, ran his hand over his regulation-cut blond hair and arranged his sermon notes.

"Right now, right at the start of today's service, I want to honor a brave young man in our church family who will be deployed this week to fight the enemies of our Lord in foreign lands. Specialist Mendoza, stand and be recognized."

The soldier stood and turned to the membership proudly accepting their thunderous applause. Carter recognized the young woman standing next to him, clapping double-time, as the same one who sat next to him on the plane. With the congregants still on their feet, the pastor called the names of two other soldiers soon shipping out to war.

"These brave young men and women not only have our gratitude but the eternal thanks of our Lord Jesus sitting at God's right hand, amen?"

"Amen!" the congregation responded with hooah-like affirmation.

"People of God, there can be no more honorable calling than to glorify our Lord by putting oneself in harm's way in defense of Jesus and his holy name. Remember what our Lord Jesus said to his apostles in the book of Matthew: *Do not suppose that I have come to bring peace to the earth. I did not come to bring peace, but a sword!*" the pastor growled, bringing the membership immediately to their feet with fervent clapping, howls and whistling.

Carter reached for a Bible in the pew bookrack and flipped to the book of Matthew to check the context of the pastor's quote, unaware of any verse attributed to Jesus endorsing war. The "sword" was, of course, used figuratively to represent the divide that family and friends might experience if they chose to faithfully follow Jesus. But to the young soldiers in the church about to go to war, and possibly never return, an affirmation of their purpose was right and appropriate, Carter thought.

He loitered in the sanctuary until the last congregant had exited then approached Pastor Goode.

"Good morning, Reverend," Carter said, shaking the pastor's hand. "Your sermon today was inspiring, thank you. Pastor, an old friend of mine, Jeff Reed, used to be the EM pastor here, about ten years ago. Did you know him?"

"No, sir, that was quite a bit before my time. I'm a chaplain at Fort Carson and fill in here on occasion. The regular pastor, Reverend Wilson, is attending the Congress today. You might speak with Mrs. Dempsey, though," he said pointing to a grey-haired African-American woman sitting at the piano. "She's the Minister of Music and has been here for ages."

"Thank you, Reverend, or is Chaplain more proper?"

He smiled. "It's all good."

"Yes, all the time," Carter agreed, returning the smile.

Mrs. Dempsey was organizing her music and notes when Carter walked over to see her still at the piano. A framed photograph of two young boys sat to the right of the music rack. She was visibly unnerved by his presence.

She quietly hummed Horatio Spafford's faith-affirming hymn *It Is Well with My Soul* rendering Carter's friendly salutation unintelligible. "Mrs. Dempsey?" She continued jotting notes while humming more loudly to compete with Carter's interruptions. Carter put his hand on her shoulder. She stopped humming and looked up at him over her glasses.

"I'm sorry, sir, were you speaking to me? I have so much to prepare before the eleven-thirty service. May I help you with something?"

"I apologize for interrupting your work. I was looking for an old friend of mine, an EM pastor who worked here about ten years ago, Jeffery Reed. Do you remember him?"

Mrs. Dempsey's look turned hard. "He hasn't been here for a long time. He left...I couldn't tell you where," she said and resumed her work. Carter sat next to her on the piano stool. She tensed.

Carter pressed. "Do you remember anything about him when he was here?"

Mrs. Dempsey slammed her hands on the keyboard. "What is it exactly you are looking for, sir? I laid my burden down with my savior years ago. I raised my two boys with respect for the Lord's holy name and the good book and they grew into righteous, God-fearing young men, praise the

Lord." Carter glanced at the photograph. She noticed. "Was he your friend, this one who led Satan into my world?"

It was time to lay his cards on the table. Carter revealed his Inspector's badge to the woman. "I have not been completely honest with you. I'm a police inspector from Minnesota here to find information on Jeffery Reed, a person of interest in a murder case back home."

She closed the keyboard fall and rested her chin on folded arms. "Reverend Reed was a strong pastor for us. I won't say the congregation loved him - he wasn't a very loveable man - more like a strict parent that you respect for tellin' you things you really don't want to hear. Avoidin' sin was usually the message of his sermons. He would tell the young girls to save their virginity for marriage and the young women to resist temptation to cheat on their husbands, especially the army wives. He was a big influence on the young people; too influential, obviously."

"How do you mean?"

"Pastor Jeff would invite boys to his house for Bible study on Wednesdays. He would talk to them about bein' righteous young men and respectin' girls as the Bible commands. My oldest son, Lawrence, would go over every Wednesday with some other boys from the church. He would be so excited when he came home and tell me all the great things that Pastor Jeff had taught him about Jesus and lovin' your God and neighbors as you love yourself.

One evening he came home and didn't say nothin'...went straight to his room. He didn't eat for two days. On the third day he didn't come down for breakfast. We called and called." She dabbed a tear. "My husband went to his room and found him hangin' in the closet with his trouser belt around his neck. The newspapers and the police let people think he strangled himself while he was havin' sex with himself but I know better. That Jeff Reed did something to him that he couldn't talk about...couldn't live with. The next day he and that Korean wife of his were gone; left without sayin' nothin' to anyone." Fighting back tears she resumed humming the hymn, accompanying herself on the piano.

Carter stood and touched her shoulder warmly. "I'm so sorry to have made you remember that painful memory."

"It is a painful memory, sir, but there is no need for you to apologize to me for rememberin' my son. He's with the Lord now, with no pain and no shame."

Carter patted her back and left the sanctuary. His one simple question had revealed that Jeffery Reed had, in fact, been employed by Second Korean Presbyterian Church and had most likely caused such devastating emotional damage to a young boy that it led to his suicide. Maybe it would be best for all concerned if he just let things go and leave it to the lawyers, jury and judge to prove Pastor Choi's guilt or innocence.

No, he could not stop now. He had traveled thousands of miles to find out the truth about Jeannie Park-Reed and Jeff Reed and as uncomfortable as it might be for those to whom he still needed to speak, it was necessary if he was to discover how and why these people were involved in the death of Dr. Kang.

Pastor Hyun spotted Carter leaving the EM sanctuary. "Hello, Mr. Carter Brand. Did you find your friend?"

"Reverend, is there somewhere we can talk?"

The pastor glanced at his watch. "I don't have very much time right now. What would you like to talk about?"

Carter opened his badge. "I am here from Minneapolis. I am investigating the murder of a member of one of our Korean churches. My office recently phoned your church to inquire about a Jeffrey Reed and was told that he had never worked here."

"Please come to my office," the pastor said right away. Carter silently followed him down a flight of stairs to his cramped office. The pastor closed and locked the door.

"Please sit down, Mr. Brand. I assume that your suspicion was verified during the EM service?"

"Not quite, Reverend. I need more information on Jeffery Reed while he was employed at Second Presbyterian. He and his wife left soon after Lawrence Dempsey's death, is that correct?"

"Yes, they did, without notifying me or the elders and they left no forwarding address."

"Do you think they left because of Pastor Reed's involvement with the Dempsey boy's suicide?"

He paused for a few moments while looking Carter in the eye. "No, not specifically." Carter waited for the Pastor to elaborate. Hyun continued, "We were in such a state of confusion and grief when he left that we did not discover for a few days that a large sum of money was missing from our endowment fund."

"How much?"

"About twenty-five thousand dollars."

"Did you report it to the police?"

Pastor Hyun shook his head, eyes closed. "No, between the theft and the Dempsey affair we did not want to involve outsiders in sensitive church matters. You see, Mr. Brand, we call it *chahng-pee* - shame. Rather than losing face over our errors we chose to say nothing. We could recover from the theft; it was not that much money. We preferred to learn from our experience and move on."

"What about the Dempsey boy? It seems to me that you had a responsibility to let the authorities know that Reed was a possible sexual predator and dangerous to young people."

"We had no proof of that, and we did not want to keep the matter open. It was better that they just disappeared, even if it cost us some money."

Carter shook his head in disbelief. "And the fact that the boy was African American played no part in your decision?"

The pastor rose from his chair. "I have told you all the facts of the matter and now I think it is best if you go. God be with you, Mr. Brand."

"Thank you for your time, Reverend. May God forgive you," Carter said and left the office.

He exited the church through the back door and walked to the front over the circular gravel driveway. He had to get out of there. He needed time to be alone with his thoughts to sort out the dark pieces he had gathered over the past week and fit them together into the puzzle of who Jeffery Reed and Jeannie Park-Reed were and what they were doing at Gethsemane Church.

When he reached the street he paused to gaze at Pike's Peak in the distance, its frozen upper reaches briefly revealed through breaks in the passing clouds then obscured moments later, leaving visible only the mountain's lush, green, tree-lined base.

CHAPTER 53 LATE COMPANY

STANDING AT THE roadside outside the Second Presbyterian Korean Church, in Colorado Springs, Carter dug into his trench coat pocket for his taxi driver's ketchup-stained business card and called the number written on the back. The car arrived five minutes later.

The driver called out to him through the front passenger-side window, "Hey, Minneapolis!" Carter climbed in. Perhaps it was the cardboard pine tree air freshener hanging from the mirror that blunted the expected olfactory assault as most of the odor from the previous trip was gone. "Headed back to the airport?"

"Nah, I think I'll stay the night. Do you know of an inexpensive motel with clean sheets?" Carter extended his hand over the back of the seat to shake hands with the driver. "By the way, the name's Brand, Carter Brand."

"What is that, British?"

"No, it was unpronounceable and too short on vowels many generations back. My great-great grandfather changed it at Ellis Island to one of the only English words he knew."

"Well I'm Solomon, Marcus Solomon," the driver said shaking Carter's hand. "Joe Lemme just reopened his inn on

Fountain. I hear it isn't too shabby. He's got a brand new lounge if you go for country music."

"Then that's where we're headed, Mr. Solomon, country music notwithstanding."

With the exception of his uncomfortable snooze at Denver International while waiting for the first flight of the day to Colorado Springs, Carter could not remember the last time he had slept away from home. He was more fatigued than tired. He needed to find some place to eat and think; some place where he could be alone but not by himself. He deposited his bag on the bed in the narrow second floor motel room and followed his nose back to the lobby in search of the source of the aroma.

The poster outside the Summit Restaurant and Lounge advertised the "Best Steak This Side of the Rockies" with Kay Klemmons and the Kountry Kings performing that evening. He requested the waitress seat him at a table on the perimeter of the dining area, just to the right of the bar, where he could be surrounded by life and still be sufficiently alone with his thoughts.

In the past twenty-four hours he had only a bagel to eat on the plane and hadn't even finished that. He was hungry but there was nothing on the menu that appealed to him, only varied selections of beef.

The waitress arrived with pen poised over her check pad. "You ready?"

"I'll just have a drink for now," Carter said, folding the menu closed.

"Two drink minimum. Policy when we have a band."

"In that case, I'll have a double Johnny Walker Black, one ice cube. Just one."

The band arrived and began setting up for the evening gig. There was a tall, heavy guy wearing an embroidered rhinestone shirt with a hollow-body Gibson electric guitar around his neck, a skinny guy with a beard and mustache sitting behind a pedal steel guitar, a stocky bass player and a similarly-built, bearded drummer, all wearing white cowboy hats and brown leather vests. The lead singer, a young woman no more than twenty-one, who Carter assumed was "Kay" with her '70's-era curly wig and frilly Nashville skirt, appeared every bit the image of a budding Grand Ole Opry star.

When his drink arrived, Carter swigged down half the glass hoping the rapid ingestion of alcohol would calm the chaos of his racing thoughts. Before he left Minneapolis he thought he had the case figured out except for the motive. That too was now clear.

His self-financed field trip had been productive. The team of Reverend Jeffery Reed and his wife Jeannie preyed on small Korean churches that were trusting and in need of the services they could offer. With her bilingual eloquence, and his American church resume, working their way into the confidence of church administrators, then helping themselves to whatever loot was available, would have been child's play.

Jeannie Park-Reed, the mastermind, knew the key to their success would be her understanding of their victims' need to avoid shame. With that knowledge they would be able to balance the amount they could steal against a price that might be paid to avoid shame. They would have to be careful about which churches they would target. The larger churches might be richer but would be more likely to check their backgrounds and most likely have a higher tolerance for shame.

Carter tossed back his remaining scotch. Jeannie Park-Reed knew the power of *chahng-pee* and the extent to which Koreans would go to avoid it like a virulent disease. Shame was worse than death - it lived on. No price was too high to pay to escape the dehumanization of shame. In Jeff Reed, who knew no shame, she had the prefect partner in crime.

The patrolling waitress stopped by his table. "You want another double Johnny Black, hun?"

"Yes, please." Carter did not consider himself a drinker beyond an occasional beer or glass of wine, but that evening it was necessary to move body and mind to another place.

"One cube again?"

"No, straight up this time."

"Can I get you something to eat with that, hun?"

"No, just the drink is fine."

Carter nibbled on peanuts left by the waitress on her last visit. He listened to the band as they finished an acceptable rendering of a Tammy Wynette standard. The tall guy introduced the band members. Carter was mistaken. The tall guy was Kay Klemmons, not the girl. It shouldn't have bothered him, but it did - just another example of being wrong about something that seemed so obvious.

A woman sitting with her legs crossed on a stool at the bar to his left caught his attention. In the dim light he could make out that she was between thirty-five and forty-five years old, about five feet-six or seven, medium-length black hair, pulled back. She was alone nursing a drink and chatting occasionally with the bartender. Jukebox music filled in for the band while they were on break. She stirred her drink between periods of surveying the tables and their occupants.

As a distraction, Carter challenged himself to find out who she was and why she was there from the evidence visible. Was she a hooker working the motel lounge concession on the prowl for young soldiers looking to enjoy a night of passion before they deployed to an uncertain future? Was she an unappreciated, aging housewife out to prove that she was still pretty enough to be attractive to younger men? Or maybe she was just bored and needed a night out away from the family.

Before he could look away, the mysterious woman caught Carter staring at her. She smiled, dropped some cash on the bar, picked up her purse and sidled off the stool. Carter turned his attention to the band tuning up for their second set.

He smelled her before noticing her take a seat at his table. The fragrance struggling to compete with the lounge's stale beer and cigarette odors suggested the application of her perfume was more subtle than what might be expected from a common working pro.

The lines in her face, deepened now by the table candle's flickering Frankenstein illumination, had not been visible at a distance nor were the heavy applications of pancake makeup spackled on her face and neck, nor were the mended tears in the sides of her skirt. But up close, he saw them now.

She parked her purse on his table. "Care for some company?"

He did want company and from his rookie rotation through the vice squad knew the usual come-ons. To avoid solicitation, the drink would be the instrument of communication in the code of the night. If she asked him to buy her one it could be regarded as an offer of sex. If he offered her the drink she would consider it a request.

Carter smirked. "Looks like the decision's already been made."

"Excuse me," she said and pushed back her chair to leave.

Carter gestured for her to stay in her seat. "I'm sorry, that was rude of me."

"A vodka martini, dry," she said as the waitress passed the table. "I've got a tab at the bar."

The band began their second set. Carter sipped his second drink and paid even less attention to his new table companion than he did to the band. She did the same. The contest of loneliness lasted into the third song and his third scotch when the woman broke the ice.

"So, I haven't seen you in here before. Just visiting Colorado Springs?"

"Yes, I'll be leaving tomorrow morning. I'm here for a bit of unofficial business."

"Unofficial? That sounds mysterious. What do you officially do, stranger?"

"I'm a cop in Minnesota," he said and checked her face for a reaction. There was none.

"OK, officer...?"

"Jones, Peter Jones," Carter said to the woman of unknown repute.

"Shirley Wright," she said, reaching over to shake Carter's hand.

"Is that your real name?"

"Yes, it is. Is yours?"

"No, not really," Carter said, uncomfortably. "I'm Carter Brand."

"Are you a country music fan?"

"No, not really."

"Then I guess I can assume that you're a guest at the motel and didn't care much about where you ate dinner tonight?"

"That would be a good guess."

"It looks like you've been doing more drinking than eating. Want to get out of here and find someplace a little more interesting - more interesting for Colorado Springs, at least?"

"I'm pretty tired. I think I'll just go back to my room and crash. I have an early flight tomorrow."

"Care for some company?" she asked again. "I really don't feel like going home tonight. My intentions are strictly honorable, scout's honor," she said, showing her right palm.

He looked at her hand. He looked in her eyes then back at her still-raised hand.

"Sure."

Carter waved for their checks. When they came, he paid for his and she for hers. He pulled a few bills from his wallet and let them fall on the table. He did not know how much of a tip he had left - it could have been two dollars or forty dollars - and he did not care. He was drifting blindly through another bizarre episode in his increasingly surreal life.

As Carter turned to leave towards the closest exit, she hooked her arm around his. He looked at her and then her arm, then curled his arm into a proper handle.

The dimly lit lounge made the light shining through the space at the bottom of the door glow bright and all Carter could think of as they passed the tables was that doom awaited him on the other side. He became acutely conscious of the people in the lounge who, he was sure, were watching him and the woman knowingly. Did they know more about who the woman hanging on his arm was than he did? Could the Korean soldier staring at them as they passed by have been a guest at his wedding that he might have briefly met on the reception line and would scandalize him to Hannah's family when he got home that night? His flesh was crawling from shame - from *chahng-pee*.

Carter's paranoia had not abated as they walked through the lobby, past the front desk and up the stairs to his room. He fumbled for his key and, try as he might, could not insert it into the lock. She steadied his hand and twisted the key. The door sprung open.

They entered the room and switched on the light. "I'm sorry I won't be very good company tonight," Carter said, plopping down on the edge of the bed. "I'm exhausted and more than a little drunk."

She sat next to him. "Don't worry. I don't feel much like talking, anyway. Do you mind if I shower before bed?"

"No, go right ahead."

Carter reached for the wind-up clock on the night table and set the alarm for six o'clock in the morning. He emptied his pockets on the dresser leaving his wallet out and in full view. He knew there was not more than $120 in tens and twenties in it and if it was gone in the morning he could dismiss it as an act of grace or chosen naiveté. Though no price had been negotiated for his sleepmate's company, he pulled out three twenties and left them on the night table.

He removed his shirt, pants and socks and tossed them onto the arm chair seat before rolling under the covers where he lay on his side facing the wall. She undressed to bra and panties and draped her blouse and skirt neatly over the back of the desk chair then went into the bathroom to shower.

Twenty minutes later she came back into the room wrapped in a white "Lemme Inn" towel. She looked at Carter, now awake sitting with his back against the headboard studying the local newspaper, then let the towel fall to the floor. She switched off the ceiling light. Through the window, the flickering green and amber light from the giant motel sign in the parking lot illuminated her path to the bed and revealed a different chapter of her life with each neon flash on her naked body. She slipped under the covers and sat next to her host.

"So, where do we go from here, officer?"

Carter tossed the paper to the floor. "To sleep. I feel like I haven't had a good night's sleep in a month."

"Why? What's been going on with you?"

"I wouldn't know where to begin. Shirley, wasn't it?"

"Yes, it's Shirley. Wherever that beginning might be, you've ended up here sitting next to me in a motel bed so you might as well get your money's worth. I'm a good listener."

"Are you religious? Do you go to church?" Carter asked.

"Yes, yes I do. Does that surprise you?"

"A little. How do you square your occupation with your faith?"

"I avoid the Old Testament like a plague. Jesus says to not judge others or they will judge you, or something like that. How about you? Are you a church-goin' guy?"

"Yes, I am."

"So, I guess you're also kinda partial to the Gospels or you wouldn't be here, right?"

"My mind really wasn't on church tonight," Carter said before realizing that his mind had been on little else.

"So, what are we doing here?"

"I'm married. I should not be here. I haven't been close to a woman since my wife left a month ago so here we are. I love my wife, Shirley, but there is no logic to our relationship. We live together, we eat together, we make love together yet our existence together doesn't seem to have any purpose; like we're simply going through the motions of life."

"What are you looking for, Carter Brand?"

"I don't know. I always thought I would know once I found it. I just want to be happy. Are you happy?"

"Me? At times. When I gave birth to my daughter I was happy. When I saw her graduate from high school and college, I was happy. Now I get my happiness and unhappiness in measured doses. I'm pretty happy right now," she said and kissed his cheek.

"Good night," Carter said as he rolled to his side and faced the wall.

Through the night, the persistent sound of the clock's tick-tock was curiously soothing; most likely a lullaby rhythm from a long-buried memory.

Carter rose before the alarm. The woman was gone. He showered, shaved, dressed and retrieved Marcus

Solomon's card from his wallet. He dialed the cell number hoping to reach him in time to get a lift to the airport. While the phone was ringing he opened his wallet's cash pocket. The money, in both his wallet and on the night table, was as he had left it.

CHAPTER 54 MINNEAPOLIS

JASON TAPPED ON Carter's office window holding a wire milk crate filled to capacity with papers, books and a pair of sneakers. His laptop computer case was slung over his shoulder. At his desk, Carter motioned for him to come in.

"You're back." Jason said with a smile, resting his load on Carter's desk. "How was the trip?"

"I was just going to find you. Do you have some time?"

"Of course I do. With the Kang case finished I've been called back to fraud investigations. Honestly, it's been great working with you, boss, and I don't look forward to spending my days busting slimy used car dealers. What did you learn out west?"

"*Chahng-pee.*"

"I don't recognize that name," Jason said when Carter's poor pronunciation made recognition of the Korean term impossible.

"*Chahng-pee* - shame. I believe that Jeffery Reed and his wife, Jeannie or Suzy, were grifters who targeted trusting Korean churches. He would create some embarrassing situation as a distraction while she grabbed the loot. To avoid scandal, the church leadership would simply write off the theft if it was not too large - and I suspect it never was - and keep the whole affair to themselves."

"That's going to be hard to prove. Choi was caught pinching cash on a regular basis, accepting kickbacks from the building contractor and owned the murder weapon, for God's sake. We were working on a murder case, right? Not larceny. If those two were only after money where does Kang's death fit in?"

Carter rose from his chair and grabbed Jason by the shoulders. "He was a fly in the ointment, pal! This was going to be their big score and then *he* showed up. In fact, by sheer coincidence, they showed up at the same church where the only person who knew who she really was happened to be a congregant: Kang, her Pygmalion. Once Kang found his long lost love had miraculously appeared at Gethsemane he couldn't leave her alone. He was on a divine mission to save his Suzy from corruption at any cost. And when he discovered Choi's regular trysts with her, he threatened to expose both of them which would derail their whole scam.

They needed Choi to be the fall guy and buy them some time when the scheme went down. I suspect it was by chance that Jeannie found the gun when she was rifling through Choi's stuff looking for his bank cards and figured killing Kang with it would be a perfect way to get rid of Kang and implicate Choi at the same time."

Jason shook his head. "But remember, the only prints on the gun belonged to Choi. And where do Ahn and Benezek fit into the puzzle?"

"Everyone at Gethsemane knew the rumors of Kang's drugs-for-sex game he was playing with his nurse. Jeannie knew that after Kang was killed they would be on the list of likely suspects. They just had to find a way of getting them to Kang's SUV and when that rendezvous didn't go as planned they had to fall back to plan B: Choi. They killed the construction guy just to keep the focus on Choi knowing we would eventually find the murder weapon. As for the lack of prints, open up your computer. Do you still have that video from the memory stick?"

"Yes, why?" Jason laid the computer on Carter's desk and switched it on. After it booted, he double-clicked the video icon still on the Mac's desktop to start the video.

"Advance it to where she reaches over to remove his rubber." Jason moved the control to the right until the video reached the point Carter requested.

"Now, stop it and enlarge it as high as it will go."

"This is four hundred percent. I can blow it up larger but it will only get more pixilated."

"This is good. Look at her hands, what do you see?"

"It's kinda hard to make out but I think she's got plastic gloves on. Do you see gloves?"

"Surgical gloves. Even if she did not take the gun that night we know she was servicing him on a regular basis and probably ran the same routine. She took the gun with latex-gloved hands and most likely stashed it in that bag with the shiny buckle."

"Boss, they have Choi's case in the bag. You're not going to get much attention with your theory even if they see the video. Remember, no significant money was taken."

"Yet. We need to find out where the large money at Gethsemane is and who has access to it and we need to do that right now."

"Oh, by the way, we got a fax from Vassar's alumni director," Jason said. "There were lots of KIMs, and even HONGs with the same first names or initials but none that matched your girl's picture. Speaking of pictures, I wanted to see if Calvin Chennault or Donald Benezek could identify Jeffery Ryan from a photograph but there were none I could find. "

"I would be surprised if there had been."

CHAPTER 55 LUNCH

THE WAITRESS at the Hungry Bear Diner greeted Carter.

"One for lunch?"

"Yes, but I'll be fine at the counter," Carter replied, while scanning the restaurant for Detective Kaufman.

From a table near the window, Kaufman waved. "Inspector, come join me."

Menus in hand, the waitress led Carter to the small booth where Kaufman was sitting, already eating his lunch. "The usual?" she asked Carter. He nodded.

"Welcome to the Fifth Precinct commissary," Carter said.

"Congrats on the Kang case. I hear it's a slam dunk. The pastor did it, right?"

"Maybe, but let me ask you. Do you recall where the church funds are deposited?"

Kaufman held up an index finger to signal Carter to wait for the answer until he finished chewing his food. He swallowed, took a gulp of milk, and wiped his mouth with his sleeve. "Let's see, most of the cash was in NorthernStates Bank where they also have a ten million dollar construction line of credit and a two hundred fifty thousand dollar revolving credit account. They also have about two hundred grand deposited at the Bancroft S&L. They make most of their bill payments and petty cash withdrawals from there. Weekly checks and offerings are deposited there, too."

"So, you didn't see any activity with CreditSuisse?"

Kaufman guzzled his remaining milk and burped. "No, there was none that I saw, but I did wonder why the account was open if they never used it."

The waitress arrived with Carter's Cobb salad and matzo ball soup. "Who has access to those accounts?"

"Only the church finance guy, what's his name, Kwon, and the pastor. You gonna eat your crackers?"

CHAPTER 56 COMMIT

A GALE-FORCE wind blew the falling snow hard against the windows at 153 Fisher Avenue and whistled through cracks in the dried and chipped weather stripping. A long ash finally fell off the end of the cigarette dangling from Jeff Reed's quivering lips and onto the computer's keyboard. With hands trembling, he signed into the Gethsemane Church escrow account on the NorthernStates Bank website, reading the login credentials character by character off a folded napkin making certain that each was correct.

Sweat beaded his forehead as he clicked the tab to bring up the screen for transferring funds between local accounts. From there, he switched to the area for moving money between a local account and an account at another bank. He took a long drag on the cigarette, incinerating it nearly to the filter.

The computer screen went blank. The room went dark. The window pane flexed and rumbled against the gusts. Jeff frantically pressed buttons and toggled switches on the computer in desperate attempts to snap it back to life. He prayed: "Lord, if there is any mercy you have left for me please, please show it to me now. Father in heaven, I beg you!"

The room lights flickered and just as quickly returned to full, steady brightness. Jeff stabbed at the computer's power button to start it up cold. The screen lit up then went completely blue with a block of white text in the center; text that probably had meaning to a computer expert but to Jeff it meant only that he was in very deep trouble. Desperately, he switched the computer off and on to get it running normally again but it was no use. Each time, the computer would begin to start up then freeze with the cryptic white numbers on a blue screen.

He cycled the computer power one more time, begging for God's grace as he released the button. It started-up and advanced past the blue screen but froze with the iconic hourglass blinking. He dropped on the floor, pulled his knees to his chest and rocked back and forth, whimpering.

The phone rang. Jeff froze. It rang again. He turned his head up towards the cordless phone sitting in its cradle on the desk above his head. The phone rang again. He reached up to the desktop and fumbled for the handset. He grabbed it, pulled it down and pressed the answer button.

The voice on the other end of the call greeted him in Korean. "*Yoboseyo?*"

"Hello?" Jeff responded.

"Iss Misses Kim there?"

"This is Jeffery Reed. Who am I speaking with?" Jeff demanded.

"Oh...this is Moon from the travel agency. I have news for your wife."

"I'm her husband, you can tell me."

"Well, OK, please tell her that her Asiana flight to Gwangju tomorrow is cancelled...the snow. Will you tell her please?"

"*Ajuma*, you must have the wrong person. We are not going to Korea. We are going to Costa Rica. You either have the wrong number or the wrong information."

"Is this the number of Kim Soo-Ji who lives at one-five-three Fisher Avenue, in Minneapolis?"

"Yes, you have the right address but the wrong person, do you understand!" Jeff screamed.

"Oh, I'm sorry...if maybe you see Miss Kim, please tell her, OK?"

Jeff slammed the handset back to its base and slumped into the rolling desk chair quaking with terror. Was it a mistake? It must be a mistake - they were going together to Costa Rica and on American Airlines, not her alone to Gwangju on Asiana. He needed to ask Jeannie what this was all about when she returned home from Gethsemane.

He crushed his empty cigarette pack and tossed it in the wastebasket, after flicking it failed to eject any of its former contents. He patted his breast pocket, located the spare pack and deftly shook out a cigarette directly to his lips.

A cold shiver ran up his spine. Strength left his legs. The unlit cigarette dropped to the floor. The message was clear: Jeannie was going to leave him behind to take the rap for ripping off Gethsemane church!

His face burned with rage, the anger directed more towards himself than Jeannie. Did he expect her intelligence and sophistication would bind her to a thieves honor? He trusted her with a confidence that allowed him to be comfortable with himself and to play the role of her husband

and to follow her wherever she led him. She had used him for purposes known only to herself and now, after ten years, the delusion would end, as would his life.

Jeannie had left Carter Brand's business card next to the computer monitor. Trembling, he grabbed the telephone and dialed the Blackberry's number. He shook another cigarette out of the pack and reached for the lighter. The door creaked open behind him. He spun around. Jeannie Park-Reed was standing in the doorway glaring at him.

CHAPTER 57 GIDO

AUTUMN EXPIRES SWIFTLY and decisively in the Twin Cities, plunging temperatures below freezing most days. The Prius's electronic console displayed an outside temperature of minus ten degrees Fahrenheit and the biting wind made it feel even colder to Carter's flesh as he emerged from the car's warmth in the Gethsemane Church parking lot just before sunup.

He never needed the church's centering presence more than he needed it that morning and he grew more peaceful with each step up the stairs to the sanctuary. Carter came to church that morning as a man with a personal need to bring his burden to his savior, Jesus Christ; to make some sense of the stops along the crazy trip he had been on since Hannah left. He was also there as a voyeur, a spy. He knew that there was a good likelihood that Jeannie Park-Reed would be there that morning as well.

When he reached the sanctuary level, he continued up the stairway to the balcony and took a seat on the front row where he could look down over the railing to the pews in the main sanctuary. The cold weather had thinned the usual group of early morning worshippers to a just a handful of the most devout, including Jeannie Park-Reed.

He could see no more than the back of her head but there was no mistaking the turquoise scrunchy that bound her shoulder-length hair into a ponytail. Her arms were outstretched, grasping the back of the pew in front of her, cradling her bowed head.

Who was this person praying so ardently beneath him? What was she praying for? Was it a prayer of petition, of thanks or confession? Carter wondered who this exceptional woman might have been if fate had not intervened to set her off on such an unconceivable course. If her father had provided for her before his untimely death would she have graduated from that prestigious Korean university and been driven by her cleverness and ambition to achieve legitimate success in life or was her character so flawed that her cunning, intelligence and ruthlessness were destined to be her undoing irrespective of her future circumstances? If she had not so drastically changed her appearance would so many doors have been opened for her; and would she have stolen his heart? Who was praying in the pew beneath him? Was it Soo-Ji Hong or the creature she invented and was now so desperately trying to abandon?

He grasped the railing with both hands and rested his forehead on his outstretched arms. "Heavenly Father," he prayed softly, "grant me the strength to do what I know I must do. Lord, through your grace I have been able to do my job over the years without significant violence. I pray for that grace to continue just a few days longer. And please, Lord, forgive my sinful mind and bless and protect my wife Hannah who is a far greater gift than I ever deserved."

Shame's Evidence

He lifted his head and looked down on the sanctuary. Jeannie Park-Reed was on her feet now and turned around, staring up towards the balcony directly at him. When their eyes met, a sad expression of disappointment on Jeannie's face was quickly transfigured into an icy glare. Carter returned the piercing look and uttered a final "amen".

CHAPTER 58 BLOOD

JASON PULLED UP to the curb outside 153 Fisher Avenue in the unmarked olive-green Ford Crown Victoria. He jumped out and ran to the back yard as Carter, waiting for him on the front steps, waved for him to cover the rear exit.

Carter paused to consider how he would go about informing Jeannie Park-Reed, the woman who he until recently adored madly, that he was there to arrest her for murder. He knocked deliberately on the front door. He waited. There was no answer. He knocked again, more firmly this time.

"Jean...Mrs. Park?" He shouted. There was no response. He twisted the doorknob. It was not locked. He creaked the door open slowly, recalling the first time he had entered 153 Fisher Avenue, Jeannie Park-Reed peeking shyly through the open crack. He pushed the door fully open.

"Mrs. Reed?" he shouted.

He located his Smith & Wesson on his belt holster and moved stealthily past the kitchen, past the bathroom and down the hall to the back door to let Jason in. Jason's Glock was drawn and ready.

Jason whispered. "I only saw one car in the driveway - an old Taurus."

"That's her husband's car," Carter whispered back.

"Jeff?" Carter shouted. "Jeff, it's Carter Brand here on police business."

Except for the droning hum of the refrigerator, there was only silence. Pressed against opposite walls, they moved quietly up the hallway towards the closed bedroom doors. Jason stepped across the hall to position himself with Carter just past Jeff's bedroom door. Carter reached for the door knob and raised his weapon to the ready position. Jason's grip tightened on his gun. Carter counted down silently in synch with Jason, "Three, two one."

Simultaneously, he twisted the doorknob and with Jason crashed his body against the door whipping it fully open. They stepped into the bedroom and scanned the interior behind the aim of their guns with quick, bird-like moves. They found Jeff lying prone on the floor, blood still flowing from a wound on the side of his head.

The smell of Jeannie Park-Reed's perfume lingering in the air told him she had very recently been there. "This just happened," Carter said.

Jason's attention was drawn to the computer monitor flashing the login screen of the NorthernStates Bank website with the message: WEB PAGE TIMEOUT DUE TO INACTIVITY. CALL CUSTOMER SUPPORT.

"They tried to move the money!" Jason shouted.

Carter noticed his business card still clenched in Jeff's hand. "Jeannie probably caught him dropping dime on her and cancelled his ticket," he said, holstering his gun. "She's not going to give up so easily after all this time and planning.

The bank login is disabled. You can bet she's going for Choi's administrator login!"

"I'll go, boss. Meet me there." Jason said, and sprinted towards the back door.

Carter called-in Jeff Reed's murder to headquarters and requested backup for Jason at forty Washburn Place. In agony from crashing through the bedroom door and reinjuring his still tender hip, he hobbled out the front door and into the Prius. Snow was falling harder now and Carter switched the wipers to a quicker interval as he sped away from 153 Fisher Avenue.

Love is the shameless lawyer who can make the absurd seem reasonable to the rational mind. With each swish of the wiper blades Carter posed to himself plausible explanations for every piece of evidence collected against Jeannie Park-Reed hoping that a different picture would emerge. What would his world look like if she did not kill Kang with Choi's gun; if she did not murder Jeff Reed; if she was not on her way to force Choi to transfer millions from the church accounts to hers; if she had not stolen Choi's gun and banking credentials after having sex with him? He banged his fist hard on the steering wheel. He blared the horn. He wailed pathetically at God. How do you cancel an all-consuming desire? How do you subordinate a raw emotion to your rational mind?

You don't. At that moment he realized his greatest desire was to have Hannah back with him, complete with broken English, cultural naiveté and constantly-puzzled looks. The time for fantasy was long past.

Carter raced down the streets leading to Pastor Choi's parsonage as fast as the Prius could travel over the wind-swept snow. He pulled up to the curb behind Jason's police car. It was dark and empty. He could see two sets of footprints tracked in the snow from the curb to the front steps. One set began at Jason's Ford, the other from Jeannie's BMW parked directly in front of it.

Before heading to the house, Carter attached a cell-enabled GPS locator on the rear bumper of Jeannie Park-Reed's car.

With the aid of his cane he made his way down the snowy walk and pulled himself up the brick steps. He called out for Jason. There was no reply. He stepped into the dark house, weapon gripped and ready. He crept slowly past the couch and entered the hallway. He saw the dark profile of a body lying on the floor. It was Jason, moaning, clutching his side. Carter knelt down and quietly called in to headquarters for medical assistance for an officer down.

"Hang on, son, help is on the way," Carter whispered.

"Be careful. She has a gun," Jason warned, weakly. "She wants his login but he keeps telling her he doesn't know it."

A gunshot rang out from the end of the hall - from Pastor Choi's room. Carter staggered down the hallway as stealthily as his wounded hip would allow and braced himself against the wall. The door to Choi's bedroom was open inward. Peeking past the door frame, Carter could see the pastor sitting on the La-Z-Boy recliner, his right hand pressed against his left shoulder to stanch the flow of blood. Choi's eyes met his and squeezed out a painful warning, too late to keep Carter from coming to his aid.

The door slammed shut behind him revealing Jeannie with a gun pointed at his head.

"Put the gun down, Carter," Jeannie said, calmly.

"You know I can't do that, Jeannie."

The wail of police and ambulance sirens drew nearer. "Carter, I knew you would come after me. We don't have much time. Come with me, Carter, we can both get away."

Carter shook his head. "For what, Jeannie? All this blood for what? A few million dollars?"

"It's my life, Carter, my life! That money brings me out of hell, don't you understand? It could let you find a life too. You can run away with me and be free. Run away with me, Carter!"

"I'm finished running away, Jeannie. This is where it ends."

Her voice broke as she sharpened her aim. "Then forgive me Carter. Forgive me and tell me you understand."

Carter looked down at Choi's shoulder now hemorrhaging freely. He turned his head toward the woman he had idolized, his soul now drained as empty as the cartridge casing that would eject from her gun after she dispatched him to the hereafter. "The blood," he whispered. "All that blood, Jeannie."

Jeannie sobbed. "Oh, Carter, without blood there can be no forgiveness, only shame. You know that," she said and squeezed the trigger.

With a last surge of life, Choi shouted "*Joo-yaaah!*" and lunged at Jeannie sending her pistol flying across the room just as it discharged, the bullet striking Carter on the right side of his rib cage. Choi slumped. Jeannie spotted her pistol across the floor. Carter saw it too and dove for it. Jeannie ran out of the room, down the hall and out of the house.

The sirens wound down as the vehicles pulled up in front of the house. Carter staggered to meet them.

"Two inside with gunshot wounds," he said to the medical technician before lunging into his car.

The paramedic called after him. "Hey, where are you going? You need help!"

Carter switched the Prius into power mode, slammed the car into gear and pulled away as fast as the hybrid vehicle would travel over the snow-slick street. With one hand on the steering wheel he fumbled for the Blackberry to bring up the web browser to display the position of Jeannie Park-Reed's BMW, a feat that was difficult for him with two thumbs, much less with one and bleeding ribs.

Through windshield wiper cycles, Carter strained to keep his car straight and in control while stealing glances at the blinking icon on the Blackberry that represented Jeannie's location.

She had raced north on Xerxes, then left onto West 84th, right on Frances, left on 76th, right on Parklawn. She had been successfully evading the police cars in pursuit since leaving Washburn Place, but even without the benefit of the GPS, he knew she was heading for the airport. Anticipating her destination, Carter took the shortest route to 494 after leaving Washburn Place knowing that she would have to eventually end up on the same road.

And she did. From his right lane vantage point, he spotted Jeannie's BMW streaking past traffic in the left lane, snow blowing wildly behind it. He accelerated to the middle lane and switched on the dashboard's rotating beacon. Cars all around slowed as the circling red beam painted their windows. Jeannie saw it too and floored the accelerator.

Carter knew the Prius was no match for Jeannie's speedy German sports car but it did not matter. She had nowhere to run.

Traffic slowed behind a salt spreader truck as she approached route 77. She blared her horn while slaloming around the slowed cars. Carter moved steadily closer until he had her in sight. The red beacon's beam wiped across her rearview mirror. She veered hard left onto 34th Avenue skidding through the intersection. The airport was just ahead.

A snowplow pulled away from Fort Snelling Cemetery directly in front of Jeannie. The antilock brakes fought her foot pressure as she jammed the pedal to the floor. The plow's raised wing tore her car's right side to shreds as she tried to swerve around it but the car's inertia shot it clear.

A smiling hound suddenly flashed into the headlights. She screamed. She spun the steering wheel crashing her streaking car into the curb where it hurtled into the air cartwheeling end-over-end-over-end until it came to rest upside down on the cemetery grounds.

Jeannie lay face up and motionless in a pool of blood on the snow, her flesh shredded from a violent ejection through the windshield. Dripping a trail of blood from his saturated shirt, Carter limped woozily towards Jeannie's body.

A pack of wild dogs approached warily and gathered around her. "Get away!" Carter yelled, hoarsely, scattering all but the lead dog who continued lapping at the snow flavored with Jeannie's blood.

"Go!" Carter shouted again, with all the strength he could muster. The dog stood its ground, defiantly. Carter frantically threw a desperately-formed snowball at the dog. It continued licking Jeannie's blood off the snow. He reached into his pocket and hurled the Blackberry at the dog striking it squarely on the rump. It hopped, growled, turned its head in Carter's direction and bared its bloody fangs. Carter drew his weapon and dropped the cur dead with a single shot through the head.

He crawled on his knees over to Jeannie's lifeless body and looked somberly at her lacerated face. He said a prayer then palmed her eyelids closed. "You're free now Hong Soo-Ji," he whispered. "May God have mercy on your soul." Then he collapsed beside her.

EPILOGUE

WITH HANNAH BY his side, Carter eased the Prius out of short term airport parking and headed towards the 34th Avenue exit. He glanced left as they passed the cemetery's snow-free lawns, Hannah's presence immunizing him from any wistful feelings.

The redeye flight had returned Hannah to Minneapolis with several hours to spare before the start of Sunday church service. "Did they give you breakfast on the plane?" Carter asked as they approached the EAT-WELL diner.

"Yes...but we can eat again. They served an egg sand-WICH that did not look very freSH."

Carter managed a smile of equal parts gratitude and shame at Hannah's effort to please him with overly-precise English pronunciations. Appreciative as he was, he wanted her back the way he had left her with all the flaws and innocence that he had come to cherish early on.

The diner was typically packed with the Sunday morning brunch crowd, requiring Carter to settle for the last vacant parking space at the far end of the lot. While walking to the entrance, he perceived a certain glow about her and a fullness of features - face, bosom, bottom - which he dismissed as the yearnings of a man too long without physical intimacy.

"Two for breakfast?" the waitress asked.

Carter confirmed with a two-fingered 'V'.

"Would you like a booth or table?"

Hannah answered first and decisively. "Booth, please."

They were led to their seats and Hannah began diligently studying the menu as soon as it was handed to her. While setting fresh utensils in front of them, an overtaxed busboy positioned Carter's fork too close to the edge of the table and it dropped to the floor.

"I'll get it," Carter said to the boy, and reached down to retrieve the fork. Poking his head under the table, he spotted the remains of a partially removed vulgarity scribbled on the vinyl seat cushion and realized that they were sitting in the very same booth where they sat on one of their first dates. It was where Carter had introduced Hannah to the existence of banana splits and advised her of the accepted American policy of limiting consumption to one per day.

"Are you two ready to order or do you need a few more minutes?" the waitress asked, hoping to process their order quickly and reduce the backlog of waiting customers.

"We need..."

"I'll have the breakfast special, please," Hannah cut in.

"How would you like your eggs, miss?"

"Scrambled, please."

"Sausage or bacon?"

"May I have sausAGE and bacon both?"

"Sure, honey, but it's extra, OK?"

Hannah nodded.

"A toasted bagel with cream cheese and a cup of coffee is fine for me," Carter said. He looked up from his menu and over his glasses at Hannah who had already started on the basket of complimentary rolls.

When their breakfast arrived, the waitress placed a collection of food-bearing dishes around Hannah and Carter's single bagel in front of him. He reached for his wife's hand and said grace - an act which caught her off-guard. After thanking The Lord for Hannah's return - and the bounteous food she was about to consume - he reached over the table to spear one of the two fat sausages lying on her plate. In a flash, she trapped his fork with her own to foil the theft.

"Did they really feed you on the plane?" he sighed.

Before answering, Hannah masticated completely her first bite of sausage and then, holding her hand in front of her mouth to block her smellish breath, said, "Honey, your children have their father's appetite."

Carter squeezed her hand and smiled.

www.ingramcontent.com/pod-product-compliance
Lightning Source LLC
Chambersburg PA
CBHW070051260626
47160CB00004B/1179